*When Lily slipp___
Mallory's, she felt that pesky lump in
her throat again.*

Emotion expanded in her chest and squeezed her
heart. This little girl meant the world to her and she
would do anything in her power to make Lily happy.

Hand in hand they walked through the store,
sticking to the main aisle. Almost at the exit leading
to the mall, there was a display of girls' fancy
dresses. Lily stopped dead in her tracks to look at
an off-white, full-skirted, sleeveless lace-over-satin
dress.

"I love this," she said.

"It's very beautiful," Mallory agreed. "But you don't
have anywhere to wear something like that."

"A flower girl could wear it." Serious dark eyes
looked up at her. "For a wedding."

Mallory's heart squeezed again, this time with an
emotion more complicated than love. How did you
protect the child you cared about so much from
something that wasn't within your power to make
happen? Even if you wanted it.

* * *

MONTANA MAVERICKS: 20 Years in the Saddle!

Dear Reader,

Have you ever been somewhere a dozen times and never noticed that certain person, then suddenly he catches your eye? Is it a sign from the universe or subconscious desire willing you to be near that man who makes your heart skip a beat?

In *From Maverick to Daddy,* this is the predicament facing Mallory Franklin. She's been through a year of changes, including taking in her orphaned niece. Letting cowboy Caleb Dalton, resident playboy of Rust Creek Falls, into their lives is not a smart move.

Caleb likes all women, and his only commitment is to staying a bachelor. But there's something about Mallory and the little girl she's raising that starts him thinking; does he really want to stay footloose and fancy-free—or go from maverick to daddy?

It's hard to believe the Montana Mavericks, with heroines we root for and maverick cowboys we love to love, has reached such a significant milestone. Without reader support this series would not still be around. Thanks for twenty years of loyalty!

Always,

Teresa Southwick

From Maverick to Daddy

—

Teresa Southwick

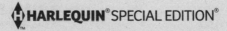

HARLEQUIN® SPECIAL EDITION®

Special thanks and acknowledgment
to Teresa Southwick for her contribution to the
Montana Mavericks: 20 Years in the Saddle! continuity.

Recycling programs
for this product may
not exist in your area.

ISBN-13: 978-0-373-65829-9

FROM MAVERICK TO DADDY

Printed in U.S.A.

TERESA SOUTHWICK

lives with her husband in Las Vegas, the city that reinvents itself every day. An avid fan of romance novels, she is delighted to be living out her dream of writing for Harlequin.

To Christine Rimmer,
fabulous plotting partner, writer and friend.
It's always a pleasure to work with you, and your
generous help on this book is very much appreciated.

Chapter One

The little Asian girl sitting at the desk where his father's receptionist normally sat was one heck of a surprise to Caleb Dalton. It was something you didn't see every day, at least not in the law offices of Ben Dalton. Cute as could be, she looked about seven or eight, going on twenty-five. A dainty, beautiful little doll.

"Hi, there," he said, politely removing his hat.

"Are you a real cowboy?" Her black eyes glittered with excitement.

"Yes, ma'am, I am."

"Cool." Her delicately shaped mouth curved into a smile for just a moment, then she was all business. "I'm sorry to tell you, but the office is closed. Can you come back tomorrow?"

"I'm pretty sure Mr. Dalton will see me anyway." The man was his father and that should get him a pass.

"Do you have an appointment?"

"Sort of." Picking his dad up to take him out for a beer should qualify.

"Mr. Dalton is doing something very important right now and can't be disturbed. You'll have to wait. Please take a seat." Little Miss Efficient went back to reading her book.

Caleb wasn't sure whether to laugh or do as he was told but finally opted for the latter, since he was in no particular hurry. And how often did a kid get to boss around grown-ups? Might be good for her self-esteem. Although from what he could tell, she was definitely not low on confidence.

Spinning his hat in his hands, he walked over to a chair against the wall and sat as ordered. The high oak reception desk where the little girl wielded power like a Supreme Court Justice separated the client waiting area from the wide doorway beyond, which was his father's office. His paralegal worked back there, too.

Here the floor was dark wood and the beige walls were decorated with watercolor paintings of mountains, cowboys on horseback and the local waterfall for which Rust Creek Falls, Montana, was named. He'd been there less than a minute when he heard the click of high heels hurrying closer, and a young woman emerged from the back office.

"I heard the bell over the door. Is someone here...?" The woman stopped short and looked at him.

The little girl glanced up from her book. "I told him Mr. Dalton was busy."

"With important business, I was told." Caleb stood and walked closer, as if drawn by some invisible force.

This woman wasn't classically beautiful, but there was something about her that intrigued him, attracted him. Maybe it was the long-sleeved white silky blouse tucked into a straight, formfitting black skirt. She wasn't very big, but the high heels made her legs look long and sleek.

"I'm so sorry. Please tell me she wasn't rude."

Spoken like a concerned mother. The little girl must be adopted. "No apology necessary."

"Lily, you should have let Mr. Dalton know his son is here."

"You told me to read and be quiet as a mouse and not get in the way when Cecelia dropped me off," the little girl protested.

"I know. But sometimes there are exceptions…" The woman sighed and the movement did interesting things to the body under that silky white blouse.

"How did you know?" he asked her.

"Know what?"

Caleb was sure they hadn't met. A striking woman like her would be nearly impossible to forget. "That Ben is my father."

"There's a picture of you in his office. He has photos of the whole family. You're Caleb, the youngest of the boys." She smiled. "He brags a little."

"Have you called him out on it?"

"All the time, but he's not intimidated."

"That's my dad." He grinned. "You have me at a disadvantage. I don't know your name."

"Mallory Franklin. I'm his paralegal. And this little girl is Lily. My niece. It's nice to meet you."

"Same here." Caleb took the slender hand she held out and his own seemed to swallow it.

He was certainly no stranger to meeting women; it happened to him on a regular basis. But this was different. She—Mallory—was different. Her auburn hair was long and shiny, spilling past her shoulders. Warm brown eyes met his and he saw easy laughter there. What was it about the combination of features that made him want to charm her straight into his bed?

There was a thought Caleb wanted to put out of his

mind. He didn't see a ring on her left finger, but that didn't mean anything. Her niece was probably adopted and he wondered why Mallory was taking care of her. There could be a husband, and marriage was a sacred line he didn't cross. Even if she wasn't, a woman with a child was a complication he didn't need.

"So, you're here to see Ben?" She looked at their joined hands and he realized he was still holding hers.

With a fair amount of reluctance he loosened his fingers. "Yeah. I'm taking him out for a beer."

"Good. He works too hard and needs to relax."

"That's what my mother says."

"I'm guessing you're going to Ace in the Hole?" One of her auburn eyebrows lifted.

"It's the only place in town. And I really mean that."

"I like that Rust Creek Falls is small," she said.

"It is that." Instead of being grateful that he hadn't met her sooner, the reminder of how small the town was made him wonder where she'd been. He refused to even add *all my life.* "You're new here."

"I moved here in January."

Since it was now August, that meant she'd been there almost seven months. "How is it I haven't seen you around?"

"I'm guessing Bee's Beauty Parlor and the doughnut shop aren't at the top of your list of places to hang out."

"Good guess," he admitted.

"What about church?"

"I go when I can. Work on the ranch keeps me busy, but on Sundays when I can't get away, I look at the mountains, trees, falls and that's my place of worship. It's prettier and more fitting than the inside of a building."

"I can't argue with that." She tapped her lip and a sly look turned her eyes the color of melted chocolate. "You probably don't get over to the elementary school much, either."

"Nope. Once a year when everyone in town pitches in to get it ready for opening day is about the only time."

"I like that small-town spirit. Lissa Roarke captured it in her blog and caught my attention. It's one of the reasons we moved from Manhattan. It's a wonderful place to visit, but I grew up and lived most of my life in Helena."

"A Montana girl." He wasn't sure why that should please him, but it did.

"Yes, sir. So raising Lily in the city didn't seem best."

"Do you miss it?"

"Excuse me. Twenty-four-hour takeout," the little girl chimed in. "I miss fast food whenever I want it. And Central Park."

He hadn't been aware she was listening. In fact he'd all but forgotten she was there. "Yeah, that's a problem. What about you, Mallory?"

"Multiplex movie theaters," she said dreamily.

"Museums," Lily added.

"Montana has been an adjustment for her. It was awfully quiet at first but she's getting used to it."

"I have a friend." The little girl smiled. "And I like cowboys. I want to learn how to ride a horse."

"I rest my case," Mallory said. "All indications are that we made the right decision moving here."

His father appeared in the doorway to the reception area, then walked over to join them. "Caleb, sorry to keep you waiting."

"No problem, Dad." They shook hands.

Ben Dalton was roughly six feet tall, the same height as Caleb. They had the same blue eyes and folks said their hair was an identical shade of brown before the older man's began to show silver. Folks also said Caleb got his good looks from his dad and a little too much charm from his mother's side of the family.

"I see you've met Mallory and Lily."

"Yes, sir."

"Best paralegal I've ever had." The older man nodded approvingly.

"It's nice of you to say so," she said, a becoming pink flush spreading over her cheeks.

"Not nice at all," he protested. "Honest-to-God truth. You're a valuable asset to this office and I appreciate all your hard work."

"And I appreciate having a boss who understands and respects family obligations. Being able to leave at five o'clock every day to pick up Lily from day care is really important to me."

"I was informed in no uncertain terms that the office was closed." Caleb looked at the clock on the wall that said it was half past six. "All evidence points to a boss who's a slave driver."

"Mallory graciously offered to stay," his father defended.

"It was an emergency," she said. "Besides, Lily isn't in school right now and Cecelia Clifton was watching her and offered to drop her off here."

Caleb began to doubt that Mallory was married because it sounded as if there wasn't a husband to pick up the slack. But that was not his problem and none of his business. "So, you ready to go, Dad?"

"Just let me shut down the office. I'll be back in a minute. Mallory, go home."

"Yes, sir."

Caleb watched Lily close her book and climb down from the big chair to stand by her aunt. The way the little girl tucked her hand into Mallory's tugged at something a little empty inside him.

"I'm glad we finally met," he said. "And your niece shows a lot of promise as a sentry. No one gets past her. You've done a great job with her."

"And she did it all by herself. She doesn't have a husband," Lily volunteered cheerfully. "But I think maybe she'd like one. Maybe a cowboy."

Mallory looked horrified. "Lily—"

"Okay, son. Let's go get that beer. Will you lock up, Mallory?" His father rounded the corner like the cavalry coming to the rescue.

Caleb wasn't about to ignore a diplomatic exit strategy when he saw it. He put his hat on, touched the brim respectfully toward the two ladies, then followed his father out the door.

He'd done his fair share of dating and then some. He'd gone out with blondes, brunettes, redheads and women whose hair was every shade in between. Ladies with blue eyes, green, black and brown had flirted and cozied up to him.

His brothers would laugh him off the ranch if he said it out loud to them, but meeting Mallory Franklin had felt like a lightning strike. No woman had ever had that effect on him before and he didn't much care for the fact that this one did. He could deal when there was a ghost of a chance that she was married, but now he knew for sure she wasn't and it was a problem. Not only was there no husband, she was looking for one.

Then again, soon enough someone in Rust Creek Falls would clue her in that Caleb Dalton wasn't marriage material.

Mallory wished she could get the look of panic on Caleb Dalton's face out of her mind. Clearly, escaping from her as quickly as possible had been his top priority. That was several hours ago; she and Lily had come home to their three-bedroom house on the southeast corner of South Broomtail Road and Commercial Street. It was after dinner, so the two of them were in the middle of the bedtime routine. Still, every time she remembered this child telling him she'd like a husband, Mallory wanted the earth to open and swallow her whole.

Nothing could be further from the truth.

She looked at the little girl, blow-drying her thick, straight black hair after her shower. This child had been placed in her care by a cruel twist of fate, making Mallory a mother. Lily hadn't come with a set of instructions or a how-to manual. There needed to be a discussion about what she had said, but Mallory didn't want to make her think she'd done something wrong or stifle her natural enthusiasm and spontaneity.

She just needed Lily to understand that she couldn't go around telling virtual strangers, not even cowboys, that her aunt was looking for a husband. But how did one approach that?

Mallory had no model from her childhood to fall back on. Her own parents would have oozed disapproval, then given her the silent treatment. She'd decided when Lily came to live with her that when there was an issue, she would do the exact opposite of what her mother and father had. So far Mallory had managed to handle every situation fairly easily, but now was definitely the time for a talk.

When the little girl turned off the blow-dryer, Mallory said, "Lily, how did you like spending time at the office today?"

"It was okay. A little boring."

Not from where Mallory had been standing. She squeezed toothpaste onto a princess toothbrush and handed it over. "Oh?"

"I like reading, but it would have been more fun at Amelia's house."

Her new best friend. "I'm sorry that didn't work out. But sometimes—"

"Things don't go the way we want and we all have to do things we don't like," she parroted.

"Right." That was good, no? Finishing the sentence proved that she listened and filed it away. "You did a very good job at the receptionist desk."

Lily stuck the toothbrush into her mouth and talked around it. "Do you think Mr. Dalton will pay me?"

Mallory laughed. "I think that was pro bono. That means you did it at no charge."

"That's what I figured." She brushed her teeth, then rinsed and wiped her mouth on the green hand towel sitting beside the sink.

Mallory was sitting on the closed lid of the toilet and stood. "Are you ready for bed?"

"Do I have to be?"

"It's time," she answered, firm but kind.

The token pushback was part of the established nighttime ritual. After Mallory's sister and brother-in-law died together in a car accident, she'd become Lily's guardian and the two of them had gone to grief counseling. She'd learned that routine would provide security and stability, a safe environment to put one foot in front of the other and get on with the business of living. It seemed to be working.

Lily turned off the light as she left the bathroom and Mallory followed her down the hall. The child's room had lavender walls with white baseboards and doors. A canopy bed was centered on one wall with a princess spread over it that matched the lamp and curtains. Her niece had picked out everything because Mallory felt it was important for her to feel as if she had some control over her life. Even if control was an illusion, a fact hammered home after the trauma of losing her mother and father at the same time.

Lily hopped on the bed and grabbed her favorite stuffed animal, a pink elephant. "I like Mr. Dalton's son."

"Caleb." Mallory cringed just thinking about him, then sat on the bed.

"I think he's very handsome. Like a prince. Can a cowboy be a prince?"

Mallory thought he was handsome, too. Brown hair, blue eyes, muscular. The white cotton snap-front shirt he wore fit him like a second skin and highlighted the contours of his broad chest and flat stomach. Worn jeans hugged strong thighs that no doubt kept him from falling off his horse while he did whatever job needed doing on the family ranch. But saying any of this out loud to Lily wouldn't be productive to this conversation.

"That depends on your definition of prince. Usually that's a male child born to royalty."

"That's not what I meant, but it's okay. You're changing the subject. You do that when you don't want to talk about something."

"Do I?" She hadn't realized Lily noticed. All her energy went into learning and knowing this child and she hadn't thought about the fact that it worked both ways. "I guess I do. But there is something I'd like to talk about."

Lily sighed. "I bet it's about what I said."

"What do you think you said?" She was a smart little cookie.

"I shouldn't have told Caleb you'd like a husband."

"That's right." She took Lily's small hand into her own and brushed a thumb over the delicate knuckles. "The thing is, ladybug, you and I have been through a lot of changes in the last year."

"You mean because Mommy and Daddy died."

"Yes." Her heart caught. Would that always happen when she thought about her only sister being gone? She couldn't even imagine how Lily felt. "You and I are getting used to each other."

"I like living with you."

"And I like you living with me, too." Her heart caught again. "But I'm really not looking for a husband."

"Why not?"

So many reasons. None of which Lily would understand. "I just think it should be you and me alone for a while. Bringing someone else in is another change and we've had so many."

"If you say so."

"I do."

Mallory knew her mother would have continued to hammer the message home, so in keeping with her philosophy to do the opposite, she figured enough said. "It's time for your prayers, sweetie."

The little girl closed her eyes and folded her hands with the stuffed animal still under her arm. "Dear God, bless my friend Amelia and her mom. Mr. Dalton and Caleb. Everyone at day care. Please take care of my mommy and daddy. Keep them company so they don't miss me too much. Bless Aunt Mallory." She opened her eyes, then quickly scrunched them shut. "I almost forgot. Mommy and Daddy, please help Aunt Mal be ready for another change. Amen."

Without commenting on the content of the prayers, Mallory leaned close and kissed the child's forehead. "I love you, Lily."

"Love you, too." She rolled away and curled into a ball. In minutes she would be asleep.

Mallory quietly slipped out of the room, then stopped in the doorway for a last protective look at the child she grew to love more every day. Reading between the lines of that prayer, it was pretty clear that Lily wanted a father. A transparent plea to replace what she'd lost.

The praying-to-a-higher-power strategy was sound, since it would take an act of God to modify Mallory's position. Relationships were trouble. She'd spent two years with a guy who demanded more of her time, then dumped her when she couldn't be at his beck and call. That was before she had a child to raise. Between her job and being a mom, she had nothing left over for anyone else.

Not even a handsome cowboy who, for just a moment, had made her wish it could be different.

After a burger and beer with his dad, Caleb drove to Crawford's General Store, a brick building that fronted North Main Street. They were out of coffee at the ranch and it was his turn to buy. If he showed up in the morning without the can, his brother Anderson would can *him*. And he'd been warned that the family connection wouldn't save his sorry ass.

He walked past the storefront window displaying an array of merchandise. It was the only store in town and this was a ranching community, so there was a variety of items from saddles to soup. If they carried what you were looking for, it would save a thirty-minute trip to Kalispell, which was the next town over and a lot bigger.

Caleb went inside, past the general-purpose aisles on his way to where the coffee was shelved. He was a man on a mission. When he found what he wanted, he made sure it was high-test with the maximum amount of caffeine, then grabbed as many cans as he could carry and headed for the checkout counter. Vera Peterson was ringing up a purchase for a young woman who looked sort of familiar.

Vera glanced up and smiled when he got in line. "Hi, Caleb."

"Good to see you, Vera." It always was.

They'd been good friends for a lot of years and he liked her husband, too. But a long time ago, before she'd even met the man she was happily married to, Caleb had a thing with her. She was a little older, a lot wiser and had taught him quite a bit. Although she hadn't been able to teach him that there was any point to love, and no one since had changed his mind about that.

The customer in front of him turned and got a big, flirty look on her face. "Caleb Dalton. Imagine running into you. It's nice to see you again."

Again? He had no idea what her name was. A brunette with hazel eyes, she was pretty and probably one of the numerous women who'd moved to Rust Creek looking for a cowboy to marry after reading Lissa Roarke's blog. Like Lily's aunt. Mallory. Now, *her* name he could remember. And chalk that up to the fact that he'd been distracted all through dinner with his dad. What was her story? Why didn't she have a husband? He didn't want to wonder about any of it but couldn't seem to turn off the curiosity.

"Would you like to go get coffee or something?"

The words from the hazel-eyed brunette pulled him back from a vision of auburn hair, brown eyes and the prettiest smile he'd seen in a long time. "Sorry?" He shook his head to clear it. "What was that?"

"Do you want to get a cup of coffee? Or something?"

It surprised the hell out of him that he wasn't interested. Not tempted even a little bit. But giving her a blunt no wasn't his style, so he prettied it up.

"Normally I'd like that, but I have to be up before God. Work on the ranch isn't nine to five."

She took her change from the clerk and picked up her bag before giving him a disappointed look. "Maybe another time."

No point in saying yes because it would be a lie. "Have a good evening."

"You, too." She walked out the door and lifted her hand in a flirty waggle of fingers when she passed in front of the window outside.

Vera gave him a what's-with-you look, then rested one hand on a jeans-clad hip and stared at him as if he was wearing a snake around his neck like a tie. "You sick or something?"

Not unless thinking too much about Mallory Franklin qualified. "Never been better. Why?"

"Duh." There was a twinkle in her big blue eyes.

"How are the kids? What are they now? Six and eight?"

"Yeah. And they're fine. But you don't get to change the subject." She tossed a long, straight strand of blond hair over her shoulder. "You just turned down an invitation from a woman. And she's your type."

"How do you know?"

"Because she's a woman."

Meaning he wasn't picky and liked them all. He couldn't say she was wrong about that. "Yeah. Weird, huh?"

"I'd say so." She rang up the cans of coffee and waited for money. "Good for you."

He gave her some bills before asking, "Why do you say that?"

"Because it's about darn time you grew up."

"Bite your tongue, Vera." He grinned. "You know that will never happen."

"Never say never," she warned. "Say hi to your folks for me."

"I'll do that at dinner on Sunday." His mother insisted on it and none of her children had the nerve to say no to Mary Dalton. "You tell John and the kids hello from me."

"Will do."

He waved, then walked out to his truck and opened the passenger door to set the coffee on the seat. What had just happened? It was out of character for him to turn down a pretty lady, because he liked them all and kept things fun. As soon as that changed, he found a way to slide out of it without hurting anyone's feelings. Everyone had a gift and that was his.

He never saw the point of taking it up a notch and never said no to a potential fling.

But that had changed tonight. Because he'd been thinking about Mallory Franklin? Maybe that was what happened when you got hit by lightning. Some people lived after getting zapped, but they were never the same. Since he liked himself just fine the way he was, he needed to watch out for storm activity and head for cover as soon as possible.

He was very good at that, too.

Chapter Two

With Lily securely buckled up in the backseat, Mallory parked her compact car in front of the Dalton house. Her boss had invited them to dinner because his wife said Mallory had been in town over six months and that length of time without having her over crossed the line into unfriendly territory. It was five o'clock on Sunday and they were right on time.

"Here we are," she announced and turned off the car.

The sound of a seat belt clicking apart came from the rear seat. "Mr. Dalton has a big house."

Mallory agreed. It was located just over the bridge and next to the creek on Sawmill Street. The two-story structure was wood and glass with a manicured lawn, neatly trimmed bushes and brightly colored flowers lining the walkway to the front door.

She'd heard about the devastating flood the previous summer when the rain wouldn't stop and the creek overflowed, wiping out a good portion of the town. The law office was still handling claims and property issues along with renovation contracts and insurance matters. Right here, right now, you'd never know anything bad had happened. Ben's house was on high enough ground that it hadn't sustained any damage and she was glad for him and Mary.

"Okay, kiddo, let's go." Mallory opened the driver's door and exited the car while her niece did the same from the rear-passenger side.

Lily looked up and down the street. "There are a lot of cars."

"I noticed."

At the front door she knocked and waited for someone to answer. That someone turned out to be Caleb Dalton. He looked as surprised as she felt, but probably his heart was beating a normal, steady rhythm, while hers was pounding abnormally fast.

"Hi." His curious tone filled in the question he was too polite to ask. *What are you doing here?*

"Caleb! Do you live here?" Lily was clearly happy to see him.

"No. Just visiting." The smile he gave her was genuinely warm and welcoming. "It's nice to see you again, Lily."

Mallory wondered if he really meant that after what she'd said during their last encounter. "Your father invited us to dinner. I didn't know—"

"That I'd be here?"

"Well, yes," she admitted.

"It's Sunday."

"I'm aware of that. It's when your father told me to be here."

Ben had mentioned the family dinners a couple of times, but she didn't really get that it was all of them every Sunday. She'd had it in her head that this was just her and Lily with Mary and Ben. No way had she expected to see Caleb.

There was an edgy expression in his eyes, but she got the feeling it wasn't about her. "What I meant is on Sunday my mother insists that the whole family be here for dinner."

"That's nice." She couldn't imagine her mother doing anything like that.

Before he could respond to that, Mary Dalton walked up and stood beside her son. "Caleb, for goodness' sake. You weren't raised by wolves. I know because I'm your mother and had a hand in raising you. Invite our guests in." The woman smiled. "Mallory, I'm so glad you could come. And this must be Lily."

"Pleased to meet you," the little girl said politely.

Lily had always been in school or day care when her boss's wife had dropped into the office. Mary Dalton was a tall, very attractive blue-eyed brunette. Trim and fit, she was wearing jeans, a plaid cotton shirt and a friendly smile. Mallory liked her a lot.

The woman sighed looking at Lily. "What a cutie you are. It's so nice to have children here. I so want a house-ful of grandchildren." The expectant look she gave her son made him squirm.

Mallory wasn't sure what to say to that but figured she couldn't go wrong being polite. "Thank you for inviting us, Mary."

She stepped back and opened the door wider. "Come in."

They did and Mallory was forced to walk very close to Caleb, which put her closer than the last time they were together at his father's office. He was very tall, muscular and smelled really good, the scent a pleasant manly mixture of soap and aftershave.

They were standing in the two-story entryway with twin staircases on either side. A brass light fixture descended from the ceiling over a circular mahogany table with fresh flowers in the center.

Mallory felt like a clog dancer in a ballet. "Ben didn't mention that this was a family dinner. I don't want to intrude."

"Nonsense. He's told me how hard you work and it's much appreciated. He'd be lost without you and that means you're like family."

"Speaking of that," Caleb said, "what about Sutter and Paige? With Mallory and Lily there aren't enough places set at the table. I can put out more."

"He means the oldest of my three girls and her husband, but you probably know that." Mary looked at her son. "Your sister isn't coming."

"But you always said if our backsides aren't here for dinner every Sunday, we better be bleeding or on fire."

"Now I'm adding childbirth to the list of acceptable excuses. She just had a baby a few weeks ago."

"Seriously? That gets her a pass?"

"It does. When you go through labor, delivery and the first few weeks with an infant up all night, you'll get a dispensation, too. Until then…"

Caleb winked at Lily. "She drives a hard bargain."

"And you're a silver-tongued devil. Always trying to charm your way out of trouble." She affectionately touched his arm. "Now I'm going to introduce our guest to everyone else." She put her hand on Lily's shoulder. "Come along, sweetie."

That left Mallory and Caleb to walk behind them. He nodded toward the other room and said, "Let's go meet the Daltons."

Mallory's head was spinning and not just from being this close to the good-looking cowboy. She was baffled by the banter between mother and son. What a concept. If her mother—or father, for that matter—were that warm and approachable she'd still have a relationship with them. But disapproval was their trademark and she was pretty sure they'd frown on Lily, who wasn't related to them by blood. This child would never go through what Mallory and Mona had growing up.

Caleb led her past a big, beautiful kitchen with stainless-steel appliances and a granite-topped island to the large family room. It had a leather sectional in front of a big screen TV mounted on the wall. Ben was standing with his other two sons. She knew them from the photos in her boss's office, but shook their hands as Mary made introductions.

The men were all about the same height, six feet give or take an inch, and the unmistakable family resemblance marked them as brothers. Anderson, the oldest, had the same brown hair and blue eyes as Caleb, but there was an air of authority and seriousness different from his brother. Travis was the middle son and had his father's brown eyes.

"Are you a cowboy, too?" Lily asked him after meeting all the men.

"I am." Travis indicated his older brother. "So is he. In fact he's in charge of the family ranch."

"Aunt Mallory didn't tell me you had a ranch."

Mallory happened to be looking at Caleb and saw his mouth pull tight when Lily called her Aunt. He'd grown tense after Lily put on her matchmaking hat at the office. Clearly he was skittish about starting a relationship with a woman who had a child.

"We have a big ranch," Travis was saying. "The Dalton family spread."

"Do you have horses?" When Travis nodded, the little girl practically quivered with excitement. "I've never been on a horse, but I'd like to—"

"Lily," Mallory interrupted, "it's not polite to invite yourself."

"That's okay." Travis smiled down at the child. "Pretty girls are always welcome."

"How come you never tell us that?"

"Because you're both irritating." Travis grinned at the two beautiful young women who'd walked into the family room from the kitchen.

Mary stood between them and slid her arms through theirs. "These are my youngest daughters, Lani and Lindsay."

Both had the Dalton light brown hair, but Lani wore hers long, and Lindsay had a ponytail.

"It's really nice to meet you," Mallory said. "I feel as if I know everyone already from all the photos Ben has in his office."

"I'm Lily." The little girl grinned up at the girls. "My name begins with an *L,* just like yours."

"That's really cool," Lindsay said with a big smile. "You're just as cute as you can be."

"So, the girls will help me get drinks," Mary said. "Mallory, we have beer, wine, club soda, soft drinks. What would you like?"

"I'd love a glass of wine." It was weird because these were the nicest people in the world, but her nerves were a little raw, as if they were tightly wound springs ready to come loose. Every time she looked at Caleb they got a little more sensitive.

"What about you, Lily with an *L?*" Lani asked. "Would you like something to drink?"

"Would it be all right if I had soda?"

Mallory nodded, but added, "Nothing with caffeine."

"Coming right up. Boys, be nice to our guests." Mary put her arms around her daughters and headed them toward the kitchen.

Mallory and Lily were standing with Travis while her boss formed a circle to chat with his other two sons just a few feet away. Caleb showed no interest in talking to her, unlike the first time they'd met. At least he'd seemed engaged until Lily told him she, Mallory, needed a husband. If that was a friendship deal breaker then so be it. Her feelings would not be hurt.

After watching Mary Dalton gather her daughters, Mallory smiled at Travis. "It occurs to me that with six kids, your mom must have been pretty good at herding. Maybe that's where you and your brothers inherited the skill."

He laughed. "It's a good theory. And she's anxious to take those talents out, dust them off and use them on the next generation of Daltons."

"I understand your sister had a baby and that's why she's not here."

"I like babies." Lily looked way up at the tall cowboy. "Do you?"

"Yes, ma'am, I do."

Mallory could almost hear the wheels turning in her niece's head and decided a preemptive strike was called for. "Travis, you should know that Lily is a budding matchmaker."

"Is that so?" He squatted down to her level. "Who are you trying to marry off, young lady?"

"Me." Mallory felt as if someone was looking at her and glanced at the other group. Caleb was staring, but not at her. The frown was directed at his brother, and when it slid to her, she quickly turned away. "She thinks I need a husband."

"Is that right?" he asked the little girl.

"Maybe." The beginnings of hero worship glowed in her black eyes when she looked at Caleb's brother. "And she likes cowboys."

"Lily!" Mallory didn't know whether to laugh or apologize. "That's not true."

Travis stood and there was laughter in his eyes. "So, you don't like cowboys?"

"No. I mean yes—" She sighed. "I'm sure cowboys are lovely people for someone who's looking for commitment."

She noticed Caleb was still frowning, but this time his gaze *was* on her. Someone should tell him to be careful or his face could freeze that way. Or stop listening in on her conversation. He was close enough to hear and didn't seem to be paying attention to what his father and brother were talking about.

"Are you aware, Mallory," Travis was saying, "that you're lumped in with all the other ladies who are affectionately known as the Rust Creek Falls gal rush?"

She cringed. This wasn't the first time she'd heard that and didn't like it any better now. "If I could have five minutes alone with whoever came up with that name they'd get a good talking-to."

"You have to admit that the population of Rust Creek has increased with an influx of females."

"So are *you* looking for a gal?" Mallory asked him, letting just a hint of sarcasm slip into her tone.

"No, ma'am, I'm not."

"And why is that?"

"I've got my reasons," he said mysteriously.

Although curious, Mallory wouldn't ask, but if any of the town's female newcomers heard him say that, from Sawmill Street clear up to the falls, there would be a line waiting to interrogate him and change his mind. Although she wouldn't be one of them.

"Turnabout is fair play," Travis said. "Are you looking for a husband?"

"No, sir, I'm not."

"Fair enough," he said, nodding. "So, why did you move here?"

Before she could answer, Mary and her girls returned and handed out drinks. Mallory took the wineglass and made sure her back was to Caleb. That turned out to be problematic because her skin prickled and she felt his gaze on her, no matter how stupid that sounded. Making something out of nothing was a flaw she was working on and now was an excellent time to practice stopping the habit.

But when she chanced a look, she caught him staring at her, and the intense expression on his face stole her breath. In her humble opinion, this was the very definition of mixed signals.

All through dinner Caleb had watched Travis put the moves on Mallory and he didn't like it, not even a little bit. He was disturbed by the feeling, because earlier he'd deliberately joined a conversation that didn't include her, then found himself wanting to hear everything she said to his brother.

Now dinner conversation was winding down and he knew table-clearing was next. When Mallory laughed at something his brother said, Caleb couldn't take it anymore.

"Travis, you're on dish detail."

"I did it last week," he protested.

"Nope. That was me. You're up."

Travis gave him a back-off look. "I don't want to neglect our guest."

Caleb didn't like the sound of that. Age might have its privileges usually, but this time it was every man for himself.

His mother must have sensed something because she stood up. "Let's stack these dishes and take them to the kitchen. Travis, Anderson, it's your turn."

"Yes, ma'am." The oldest of the three brothers stood and took his sisters' plates.

"I'll entertain our guests." Caleb looked at his brother and dared him to argue. "I'll give them a tour of the garden."

"Do I have to go?" Lily was sitting between his sisters. "I'm going to play a game with Lani and Lindsay."

"Of course you can do that." Mallory's voice was quiet, but her expression showed equal parts unease and confusion.

Caleb was confused, too, and didn't get his own behavior. All he knew was that he didn't want his brother alone with her. He stood and walked around the table, then put his hands on her chair to slide it back so she could get up. Just in case Travis was planning a play, Caleb put his hand at the small of her back and ushered her out of the dining room. He guided her to the French door in the kitchen and opened it for her to walk outside.

The sun was low in the sky and would soon disappear behind the mountain. A light breeze carried the fragrances of roses and jasmine.

Mallory looked at the brick-trimmed patio and expanse of grass, bushes and flowers outlining the yard. Her gaze settled on the white gazebo in a far corner. "This is really beautiful."

"Yeah. The folks really like it out here."

"I want to do this in my yard. For Lily. There hasn't been time yet since moving. Getting her settled was the priority and it was winter. Then spring arrived, but there was so much going on at work, people picking up the pieces of their lives after the flood."

"Now we're facing down another winter," he said. "But when you're ready, I can recommend a good landscape contractor."

"That would be great." She looked as if his being nice was unexpected.

He probably deserved that. "No problem."

She walked across the grass to the gazebo and looked longingly at the wooden bench that lined the interior. "Is it all right if I sit?"

"Sure."

She did and said, "This is so lovely."

"Yeah." But he was looking at her face. Instinct had him wanting to sit beside her but he held back, leaned his shoulder against the solid support beam beside her.

"You didn't know I was coming to dinner, did you?"

That was direct and he liked her for it. No beating around the bush. "I didn't know"

"When Ben invited me, he didn't say that the whole family would be here."

"If you'd known, would you have come?"

She thought for a moment, then nodded. "Your father never misses a chance to say what a good job I'm doing. He treats his employees and clients with respect, as if they really matter, and understands that real life sometimes has to come first. It would have been rude and ungrateful to turn down his invitation."

"Are you sorry you came?"

"No." She met his gaze. "Your family is wonderful and you're lucky to have them."

He thought of Travis and thought sometimes not so much. "If you say so."

"I do." Her voice was wistful. "I wish I'd had that kind of warmth and closeness growing up."

Lily called her "aunt," so she hadn't been an only child. "But you have a sibling."

"A sister. Mona left home as soon as she was old enough, so we weren't that close." Sadness filled her eyes. "She died almost a year ago. Now I feel guilty for not making more of an effort to stay in touch."

"Lily is her daughter." Obviously the little girl was adopted. Obviously now her aunt was her guardian.

"Mona and her husband, Bill, were college professors at NYU. They couldn't have children, so they adopted Lily from China."

"Not New York?" That got a small smile, as he'd hoped.

"There, too. I couldn't believe it when I got the call that her parents were killed in a terrible accident. Hit by a taxi."

"I'm sorry." It was automatic, but he meant the words.

"Thank you." She sighed. "It just occurred to me how odd that is. Thanking someone who feels sorry for you."

"Not you," he clarified. "I'm sorry you had to go through something so terrible. I can't imagine losing one of my sisters or brothers. Even Travis."

"He's a teddy bear."

"More like a pain in the neck. But I'm related to that pain in the neck." He sat down on the bench beside her, not touching, but close enough to feel the heat from her body, smell the sweet scent of her skin. "I can't imagine what it'd be like without him."

"Cherish the closeness." She rubbed her arms as if suddenly cold. "Now there's no chance Mona and I can ever be that way."

"But you're Lily's guardian. That has to count for something. You're the one she trusted with her child."

"I appreciate you saying that. It helps."

"So, why didn't you stay in New York?" He was curious to know everything about her and liked hearing her talk. The voice that was a little honey with a side of gravel scraped over his skin and scratched its way inside.

"For a lot of reasons. It's expensive and there were sad memories for Lily everywhere."

"Out of all the places you could've come, why Rust Creek?"

The look she gave him was wry. "I admit to reading Lissa Roarke's blog, but I'm not here to find a man." The tone was a little emphatic, a lot defensive. "I liked the community spirit. Everyone pulling together after the flood and during rebuilding. Lily lost so much and I thought it was important for her to feel a part of something bigger than just the two of us. Not so alone and maybe a little more secure."

"She's pretty lucky to have you."

Rays from the setting sun brought out the red in her auburn hair and made her sad smile angelic. "That's nice of you to say."

"Not nice. Just the truth."

"Still.,"

She looked down and her long, silky hair fell forward, hiding her face. It took every ounce of willpower not to bury his fingers in all that softness and slide it back to see the beautiful curve of her cheek.

"Caleb, I didn't mean to dump all that on you. Here I am going on and we hardly know each other."

The devil of it was that the more he found out, the better he wanted to know her. "For what it's worth, Lily is a great kid. She seems to be really well-adjusted."

"Guess I must be doing something right." She shrugged. "Starting with finding a job at your dad's law firm."

"Yeah, he's okay."

"Trust me. Not every boss would invite an employee home to dinner." She smiled. "You have an extraordinary family and that's something Mona and I didn't have. It's the model for what I'd like to give Lily."

"Speaking of her…" Caleb stood abruptly. "We should probably go inside and check on her."

She blinked up at him, then nodded. "Of course."

That could have been more smoothly done but he was acting purely on survival instinct. And he was really doing her a favor. He'd enjoyed being with her and wasn't ready for it to end, but staying wasn't fair to her. She might not realize it yet, but a husband would be part of the family she wanted for her niece. That was significant and he wasn't anyone's idea of a significant other. He was the good-time guy who didn't do serious.

Not even when a woman was as pretty and tempting as Mallory Franklin.

Chapter Three

"Lily, maybe your book is at home."

At five-fifteen on Monday Mallory picked her niece up from Country Kids Day Care. After a brutal day at work she was so ready to get home. They were buckled in the car and ready to head in that direction when the little girl had told her about the missing book.

"No, Aunt Mallory. I thought I left it at school, but it wasn't there. The last time I remember seeing it was at your office."

"I can look for it tomorrow." She turned right out of the parking lot and headed north on Pine Street.

"But I want to read after dinner."

"What about reading something else?"

"I have to finish it before I start another one."

Of course. Mallory should have thought of that. She took a deep breath and pulled together the tattered edges of her patience. There were so many things she loved about being a single parent, but this wasn't one of them.

"Okay," she finally said. "I'll stop there and we can run inside to take a look around."

"Thank you."

"You're welcome, sweetie."

When she stopped for a red light, Mallory glanced in the rearview mirror and the big smile on the little girl's face tugged at her heart. Getting home required a series of left and right turns, basically a square that would take them to the bridge that crossed Rust Creek. The route took them close to the office and wasn't that far out of her way. Definitely worth the minor detour to see Lily happy.

When the light changed, Mallory took Pine Street north and made a left onto Sawmill Street. One block down was a two-story wooden building with a western facade. The weathered sign on top said *Dalton Law Office* in bold black letters. She drove into the small paved parking lot and beside Ben's car saw a four-door F-150 truck that she recognized. Just yesterday she'd seen it in front of her boss's house, and since they all worked on the ranch, one of his sons was probably the owner.

Some rogue part of her brain acknowledged which of the Dalton men she was hoping for, but she chalked it up to a completely involuntary reaction.

"Let's go find your book," she said to Lily.

They walked into the reception area at the same time Caleb Dalton was coming through the doorway of the back office. Just the Dalton man she'd hoped to see.

"Caleb!" Lily apparently didn't mind seeing him again, either. "What did you forget?"

"I'm not sure what you mean." His puzzled gaze lifted to Mallory's.

"Lily can't find her book," she explained. "She thinks she left it here the other night when I worked late."

"I remember." He winked at the little girl. "When you filled in for the receptionist."

Lily nodded. "I'll go look for it."

"Try the break room, sweetie. If Jessica found it on her desk, she would probably have put it there, then forgotten to say something to me."

"Okay. Be right back." She disappeared through the doorway.

Mallory expected Caleb to politely say *Nice to see you* and walk out the door. When he didn't, she felt the awkward silence. Last night she'd told him a lot about herself, which wasn't like her at all. He'd been understanding. Supportive even. Just when things had been most comfortable, he'd abruptly suggested they go back inside. Probably she'd shared more than she should have. TMI—too much information. Once burned made her hesitant to say anything now.

Except…she'd been working here for six months and had never seen him in the office until three days ago. Coincidence? Probably.

"So what brings you here today?" she finally asked.

"Ranch business." He nudged his black straw Stetson a little higher on his forehead. "Anderson has a new cattle sale contract. He wanted Dad to look it over before he signs and was too busy to bring it into town. I volunteered to save Dad a trip out to the ranch."

"I see." What she saw was that he'd arrived in his father's office after five, when she was supposed to be gone for the day. There was only one way to interpret that—he was avoiding her.

They looked at each other and she felt the need to say something more but everything that popped into her head sounded stupid. *I had a nice time last night at dinner. It was great talking to you. Why did you go out of your way to get me away from Travis, then take off like I was on fire?*

Fortunately Lily came back and all of those stupid statements stayed in Mallory's head. Looking closer, she noticed the little girl was empty-handed.

"I don't see your book."

"It's not here." She looked up at the tall man beside her. "But at least I got to see Caleb."

Apparently the wanting-to-see-Caleb condition was turning into a family epidemic.

"You got that wrong, little bit." He gently tapped her cute button nose. "I got to see *you*."

He got points for making Lily smile as if she felt really special. If the moonstruck expression on her face was anything to go by, the little girl was half in love with him. That was okay because Mallory would protect her.

"Okay, ladybug, it's almost time for dinner. We have to get home."

"Aunt Mallory, I have a great idea."

Uh-oh. That could mean anything from *Can we get a puppy?* to wanting takeout from her favorite place in New York.

"What?" she asked patiently.

"Caleb should come to our house for dinner. You always say we have to return the favor. It's the nice thing to do, since his mom and dad asked us over last night."

There was no way to explain the invitations weren't reciprocal, but surely he could use a diplomatic way out. "It's really sweet of you to think of that, Lily, but Caleb probably has plans."

"Do you?" Lily glanced up at him.

The easygoing charm in his eyes disappeared when he looked at Mallory. "No."

Well, darn. He didn't take the bait, so she needed to give him another hint. "We're just having hamburgers. I'd have planned something better for a guest."

"Do you like hamburgers?" the little girl asked him.

"I can't tell a lie. It's one of my favorites."

Double damn. That left her between a rock and a hard place. It was up to him now. "Would you like to come over for dinner?"

"Please say yes," Lily begged.

He looked at her. "If it's okay with your aunt, I'd like that a lot."

What could she say? "It's fine with me."

Mallory was surprised he'd agreed, but had no illusions it had anything to do with her. He probably felt sorry for Lily and that was okay. It wasn't smart, but she liked him, even more for not disappointing a little girl who'd already experienced more disappointment than any child should ever have to.

Caleb followed Mallory's compact car until she turned onto Broomtail Road and pulled into the driveway on the corner, where he parked his truck at the curb in front of the house. It was dark green with white trim and must have been newly painted and renovated because this part of town had been flooded and badly damaged after the storm last summer.

He got out of the truck and walked up the cement path that bisected the grass all the way to the porch and front door. Mallory had unlocked it and Lily must have gone inside.

"So, this is your place."

"Be it ever so humble… Please come in. Wait—" She stepped in front of him and he bumped into her, automatically taking her arms to steady her.

Also automatic was the instinct to pull her closer, lower his mouth to hers and kiss her until they were both breathless. With an effort, he pushed the thought away. "What?"

"Remember we weren't planning on company. It's usually neater than this, so don't judge."

"Heaven forbid." He held up his hands in surrender to

her terms. "Trust me, no one ever uses the words *Caleb Dalton's house* and *neat* in the same sentence. You'll get no judgment from me."

But he could certainly judge how good she smelled and the softness of her skin, not to mention all the sexy curves that her navy crepe slacks revealed. And the silky blouse tucked into the waistband outlined her breasts in a very interesting way. The devil of it was that he was normally attracted to willowy women and she wasn't one of them. And that was becoming a problem, because since meeting Mallory Franklin, there'd been nothing normal about his behavior.

Case in point: he was here.

Lily's voice carried down the hall and got to them just before she did. "I found my book. It was under the bed."

"I'm so glad." Mallory set her purse and keys on a table by the door. "Caleb, would you excuse me? I'd like to change before cooking."

"Sure." He could use some distance from all the sensual vibes she didn't even know she was giving off.

"Lily, you entertain Caleb. Offer him something to drink."

"Okay. I'll show him around."

"That's a great idea." She disappeared down the hallway to the right, then there was the sound of a door closing.

"So, this is the living room." Lily pointed to the room across the entryway. "That's the dining room."

Caleb sort of figured that, what with the cherrywood table, six matching chairs and a china cabinet. When Lily grabbed his hand to tug him along, there was no choice but to go.

Straight ahead was the family room with sofa and love seat covered in a sturdy green material. A flat-screen TV was mounted on the wall. The adjacent kitchen had white cabinets, black granite countertops and stainless-steel appliances.

"This is the kitchen and family room."

"I'd never have guessed," he teased.

"You have to see my room. Aunt Mallory let me pick out the colors and everything."

He followed her down the hall, and across from the closed door was the girliest space he'd ever seen. Light purple walls, pink comforter and matching canopy and frilly pink lamp. White trim, door and shutters blunted the color, but not by a lot. The shock of all that pink nearly made him forget that just across the hall Mallory was taking her clothes off.

Lily looked up at him. "There's another room with a computer, but it's kind of boring. Would you like something to drink?"

"Yes." He glanced once more at the closed door and knew he needed lots of ice to take his temperature down a couple notches.

He had a glass of iced tea in his hand when Mallory walked into the kitchen. The sexy sight of her barefoot in white shorts and a green tank top nearly blew the top of his head off. Her legs weren't long, but they were really nice and would wrap just fine around a man's waist.

He took a long swallow of his drink and waited for the blood to route back to his brain from where it was headed now south of his belt. "Nice place you've got here."

She opened the refrigerator and glanced over her shoulder. "Thanks. After the flood, it was in bad shape and someone walked away, so I got it for a great price. It needed a lot of work, but I could see the potential."

"My room is the best," Lily said, sitting in one of the stools on the other side of the island.

"I'm glad you think so, ladybug. Can you set the table for three?"

"Okay." She slid down from her tall stool.

Mallory set frozen hamburger patties, buns and all the trimmings on the granite-topped island beside where Caleb was standing.

The look she gave him was wry. "She likes pink."

"I noticed."

She separated the frozen patties. "It looks like a bottle of Pepto-Bismol exploded in there. I would never tell her that because the room makes her happy."

"Making her happy is obviously important to you."

"Her whole world was destroyed and I'm trying my best to put it back together." She shrugged. "There was money from her parents' estate and I thought using some for a house was a good investment in their daughter's future. It's a solid foundation for rebuilding her life. If lavender walls give her security, then that works for me. If she changes her mind and wants pink next week, I'll hire painters."

"That's quite a commitment. Not just anyone would drop everything for a kid."

Mallory watched the child put out place mats, plates, utensils and napkins. "She's given me so much more than I have her. I love her more every day. She comes first."

He'd figured that. Whoever Mallory let into her life would also be held to that standard. It was a lot of responsibility. Caleb wasn't that guy and was pretty sure she knew it, but he could be her friend. And Lily's.

"What can I do to help?" he asked.

She was cutting up tomato, lettuce and onion, arranging the slices on a plate. "Can you light the grill?"

"Hey, it's me." He grinned. "Fire good. How do you think we eat on the trail?"

"I'm guessing that has more to do with sticks and a match than propane," she said wryly. "But if I had to guess, I'd say beef jerky and MREs—meals ready to eat."

"That's just crazy talk to trash my reputation. I respectfully request the opportunity to redeem it."

She looked up, onion in one hand and knife in the other. "Just how will you do that?"

"Put me in charge of cooking the hamburgers. I promise not to let you down."

"Really? Completely?"

"Yes. Requesting permission to season the patties and be in charge of cheese."

"Wow." Amusement brought out the gold flecks in her brown eyes. "You take hamburgers pretty seriously."

"It's beef, this is Montana, and I'm a rancher. Enough said."

"Permission granted. Do I need to salute?"

"Just this once you get a pass."

She smiled, then pulled a long-handled metal spatula from the drawer and put it on the platter with the patties and cheese. "I'll make a salad and open a can of beans. The rest is up to you."

Caleb found the grill on the wooden deck just outside the kitchen's sliding glass door. After lighting it, he cleaned and prepped the grill.

Lily came outside. "Can I watch?"

"Sure. Just don't get too close and burn yourself."

"I won't."

He threw the meat on and closed the lid, waiting for the sizzling and smoking to start. In spite of his teasing, very little skill was involved in cooking burgers and Lily kept up a running commentary while he flipped and checked. There was a time when he'd have thought all the chatter would make his ears hurt, but she was sweet and funny and cute as could be.

When the patties were cooked all the way through, he put them on a plate. Lily opened the slider and he brought everything inside, then set it on the table. "Mission accomplished."

"Smells good. Mmm." Mallory closed her eyes and drew in a breath. "I'm starving."

Caleb drew in a breath, too, but for different reasons. The realization hit him like a wrecking ball that he was hungry, too. But it had nothing to do with food and everything to do with thoughts of her that he couldn't seem to shut down. This was getting more complicated than he'd expected. The dinner invitation had caught him off guard. That was the only explanation for why he'd accepted. On the drive over he'd rationalized that it wouldn't be a problem. He'd been wrong.

Now he needed to get out as soon as possible. Right after dinner, if possible.

"I think we're ready. Lily, did you wash your hands?" Mallory looked at the little girl, the mom look Caleb remembered from his own childhood when no rebellion would be tolerated.

"I'll do it now." She went to the kitchen sink and stood on tiptoe to do as ordered.

When she was finished they all sat at the table and put the stuff they wanted on their burgers. Caleb wolfed his down, but Mallory and Lily ate at a snail's pace. That probably had something to do with all the talking. Sharing details about the day. What they were going to do over the weekend.

In his little house not too far from the ranch, mostly he ate dinner by himself. Sometimes there was a woman, but he could truthfully say there were no children. This was new and felt as different as walking on the moon.

Finally the two of them had eaten until stuffed and he was nearly home free. He would wait an appropriate amount of time, then plead an early start to his day tomorrow before taking his leave. It was only polite to help with cleanup, so he and Lily cleared the table while Mallory put away leftovers. Plates and utensils were stacked in the dishwasher and counters cleaned off. He was about to say good-night when Lily clapped her hands.

"I have an idea. We should play a game." She looked at her aunt. "It's not bedtime."

"You're right. What game did you have in mind?" Mallory asked.

"Caleb, do you like word games? Like Scrabble? Aunt Mallory just taught me to play and it's my favorite!"

He'd been told he was pretty good with words, but that had to do with charming the ladies, not keeping score and tallying up the numbers on tiles. The thing was, if he said no, she would come up with something else. Best to tell the truth, then follow that quickly with how disappointed he was that he couldn't stay.

"I do like word games," he said, "but—"

"Me, too." Sheer joy and excitement glowed on Lily's face. "I'll go get the game."

After she raced out of the room, Mallory met his gaze. "Seriously, Caleb, you don't have to play."

There was something in her eyes, an expression that said she expected him to go, was ready for him to let them down.

It was the damnedest thing, but now he just couldn't do it. "That's okay. I'd really like to stay if that's all right."

The corners of her mouth slowly curved upward into a smile. "She'd really like it if you did."

An hour and a half later, Caleb shook his head after losing badly. "Lily, I think you cheat."

"No." But there was mischief in her eyes.

"You make words up," he accused.

"Maybe," Mallory said smiling sweetly, "you're better at grilling burgers than Scrabble."

"You're probably right." He stood and headed for the

front door. "I really need to get going. Work starts early on a ranch."

"Could I help sometime?" Lily begged.

"That's a conversation for another day," her aunt interjected. "It's time to get ready for bed. Say good-night to Caleb and get started, ladybug."

"Okay." She threw her arms around him in a hug, then looked up. "Good night. Thanks for coming to dinner."

"Thanks for having me."

After the little girl headed down the hall, Mallory opened the door and leaned against it. "That meant a lot to her, Caleb. It was nice of you."

"I had a great time. In spite of the fact that your niece cheats."

"Competitive and ruthless." She laughed. "It was very sweet of you to humor her. Thanks, Caleb. Good night."

"'Night." He put his hat on, then stepped out onto the porch.

The door closed behind him and he had the strangest feeling. He'd been antsy to get going and now that he had it felt like being out in the cold. In the end he'd really enjoyed himself, except the part where he kept thinking about Mallory without her clothes on.

That was damned inconvenient.

Every other Friday after work, Mallory took Lily to Bee's Beauty Parlor for a pedicure—special girl time. Sally Cameron, the operator who always did their toes, was somewhere in her twenties, a pretty brunette with big green eyes. She always knew the latest Rust Creek Falls gossip about what couple just broke up and who was going out with who. Although Mallory had told her sad story about getting dumped two years before, Sally never quite believed she wasn't interested in dating.

She and Lily were lounging side by side in the big

chairs, dangling their feet in warm, swirling water. Sitting on a low stool, Sally leaned over Lily's foot. Apparently the signal for spilling news was when she lifted the little girl's foot out of the water and started to remove the old polish.

"So what's new with you, cutie?"

"I get to ride a horse," she announced proudly.

"That's not for sure," Mallory reminded her.

"Almost for sure." There was no raining on this child's parade. "Travis said I could and he owns the ranch."

"Travis Dalton?" Sally asked.

"Yes," Lily said eagerly. "Aunt Mallory works for his dad and he invited us to dinner. We met everyone. Mary, his wife, and Lani and Lindsay and Anderson. He's the oldest and always looks like this." She sat up straight and folded her arms over her chest, then put on a very serious face.

Mallory laughed. "He's awfully good-looking but does come across a little stern. I suppose it comes with the territory—being the oldest, responsible and in charge of ranch operations."

"Think about it." Sally was using nail clippers and didn't look up. "He's not only got to ride herd on horses, cattle and other ranch employees, but also Travis and Caleb." She looked up for a moment. "Don't get me wrong. Those two are really good at their jobs, but younger brothers are always going to challenge your authority. They look for any weakness, then take advantage."

To get comfortable, Lily shifted in the big leather chair. "I met Caleb first at where Aunt Mallory works."

Mallory was still trying to forget what her niece had said to him that day. "He was there to take his father out for a beer."

"Then," Lily went on, "at his dad's house I met Travis." Sally was using the file to smooth rough edges. "He's my personal favorite. What with all the women flocking here to Rust Creek, I keep waiting to hear someone has snatched him up. A shotgun wedding wouldn't be a surprise. Or an elopement. So far, nothing."

"He's really nice," Lily agreed. "But I'm not sure who I like best. Travis talked to Aunt Mallory a lot and then Caleb looked kind of mad. He took her outside to see Mr. and Mrs. Dalton's backyard."

"Really?" Sally looked up, the prospect of interesting gossip glittering in her eyes. "Alone?"

"We just talked."

"About?"

"This and that." Mallory had no intention of fueling the fire. The man was her boss's son and there had to be boundaries. But he sure was easy on the eyes and comfortable to talk to.

"The next day," Lily continued, "he came over to dinner at our house."

"Oh?" Sally opened the bottle of cotton-candy polish, the bright pink shade the little girl loved. She started painting her toes. "How did that happen?"

"We saw him at the office again and I invited him."

"Do you think it's odd that you've been in town for six months and had never met him, then suddenly he's there all the time?"

Mallory had thought about it but couldn't come up with an explanation. "Just coincidence, I'm sure."

"Maybe, maybe not." Sally glanced up. "Hey, did you see the flyer up front advertising a lecture by Winona Cobbs?"

"Who's she?" Lily asked.

"A character, that's for sure." She laughed. "No one really has any idea how old she is, but my guess is somewhere in her nineties. And she knows things."

"What things?" Lily's eyes widened.

"Just things no one can explain. She says she's psychic and that's what the lecture is about. Everyone in town is going. You should come."

"I'll think about it." Mallory was glad the other woman had changed the subject to something other than Caleb.

"So Caleb accepted your invitation to dinner."

Somehow Mallory managed to hold in the groan. To react in any way was, in itself, fodder for town talk, so she remained neutral. "The poor man was trapped. He couldn't say no."

"Oh, he could have." There was a knowing look in Sally's eyes. "Trust me."

"He cooked hamburgers and played a game with us after dinner," Lily cut in.

"Sounds like he got pretty comfortable." Sally finished putting the clear top coat on the little girl's toes. She helped her get out of the chair without nicking the still-wet polish and said, "You know the drill, sweetie. Go to the station up front and stick your feet under the light. Let those little piggies dry."

"I will. Thanks, Sally."

"You're welcome." She pulled a clean set of pedicure tools from the little table beside her, then lifted Mallory's left foot from the swirling water. "Now that little ears are occupied, I'm going to give you some advice."

"Is it included in the cost of the pedicure?" Mallory was trying to lighten the mood.

"Just remember it's worth what you paid for it. Also that I care about you."

"This sounds serious."

"It is." She lifted her gaze. "Caleb Dalton is a notorious charmer who's too good-looking for any woman's peace of mind."

Mallory decided not to admit that she'd fallen into the typical category where he was concerned. In her humble and objective opinion, he was both charming and way above average in the looks department.

"The thing is," Sally went on, "he's never stuck to one woman for any length of time. It's always superficial and then he moves on. No one can figure out how, but his exes are all still friends."

"I'm not sure whether you're warning me or singing his praises."

"Both," Sally admitted. "He doesn't feel the need to be with one woman when he can have them all."

"I see." She watched as the woman shaped her nails, then trimmed the cuticles. She needed to respond to the statement, but waited until she was sure her voice would be normal, nothing to give her away. Because the truth was that when Caleb was around, she smiled more, glowed just a little and felt a flutter in her heart that took the edge off monotony in life.

"I appreciate the warning, Sally, but I'm not looking for anyone. It's been pointed out that I got to Rust Creek at the peak of the gal rush, but it wasn't about finding a man."

"Okay." The other woman buffed her toenails. "What with you being a newcomer, I just thought you should know."

Mallory smiled, then held still for the polish. When that step was finished, she swung her legs to the side so as not to smudge her freshly painted toes. After handing over her credit card to pay for the pedicures, she joined Lily at the nail-drying station. There was a clear plastic holder with the flyers Sally had mentioned. In bold letters at the top it said Embracing Your Inner Psychic.

She took one of the papers that had all the information and put it in her purse. Although she didn't believe that anyone could see the future, if the whole town was going, she would, too. That was what you did when trying to belong.

And wouldn't it be nice to know what was yet to happen? Mallory thought as an uninvited image of Caleb's roguish grin popped into her mind.

Maybe sometime in the *near* future that foolishness would stop. She really hoped so.

Chapter Four

In church on Sunday, Mallory and Lily listened to Pastor Alderson finish his sermon and make announcements. The last one was about the pancake breakfast fund-raiser being held directly after services.

"Some of our neighbors still need assistance to rebuild homes and businesses damaged by last year's flood," the pastor said. "We need to open our hearts and give as generously as possible to get folks who are still struggling back on their feet. See you there."

Everyone in the packed community church stood and filed out the back door.

"Can we go to the breakfast?" Lily asked. "I like pancakes."

"Of course we can." Mallory gently squeezed the small hand tucked into hers, then held on tight as they were swept along with the crowd.

They slowly moved to the multiuse room where the fund-raiser was being held. At the door was a table where volunteers were taking money and handing out tickets.

"Hello, Mallory." Thelma McGee, an older woman who had taken in many people displaced by the disaster, waved them over. Beside her was a metal cash box for the money collected. Her son, Hunter, had been the former mayor of Rust Creek Falls and the only casualty of the flood. A tree had fallen on his car, and the speculation was that it startled him into a massive heart attack, killing him instantly.

It had been a year since the tragedy, but sadness still clouded the woman's eyes. Mallory couldn't imagine losing a child and squeezed her niece's hand again. "It's nice to see you, Thelma."

"You, too." Thelma smiled at Lily. "And you just get cuter every time I see you, young lady."

"Thank you." Lily smiled shyly. "We're here for breakfast."

"And I'm here to take your money," the older woman said.

Mallory paid the asking price and received two tickets. She hadn't been here during the disaster, but this was her town now and help it she would. She handed over a twenty-dollar bill. "Just to help a little more."

"That's very generous, dear."

"It's the least I can do. I wish it could be more."

"Everything helps," Thelma said. "Go on in now and enjoy."

"Thanks, we will."

The room was big and square, with a stage at one end. She'd heard that during the crisis, cots were set up in here so that people who couldn't get into their homes until the water receded would have a warm, dry place to stay. Today the space was filled with long tables and folding metal chairs. On the other side of the room was an area set up buffet-style for food and keeping it warm as everyone filed by and helped themselves.

"Let's find a place to sit before we get plates," Mallory suggested.

"Maybe Amelia and her mom are here." Lily looked around, then smiled and pointed to a table. "There's Caleb. We can go sit with him."

Bad idea. The thought was followed quickly by surprise that he'd attended church even though he'd told her he sometimes did. She was being uncharitable, which showed how much good the church service had done her. Liking women and having them return the favor didn't qualify as cause to think the worst of him.

No matter how much she wanted to paint him as a one-dimensional playboy, he always seemed to say or do something that added evidence to support the fact that he had many more layers than she wanted to give him credit for. It also seemed that in the few times she'd been exposed to him, his charm had worked its magic on her, just like it did on other women.

Before she could come up with an alternate seating arrangement, Lily had taken off in Caleb's direction and Mallory had no choice but to follow.

She stopped behind the little girl, who was standing at his elbow. "Hi, Caleb."

"Hey there." He stood up politely. His hair was neatly combed and the cowboy hat was nowhere in sight. He smiled at Mallory. "I figured you wouldn't be far behind."

Although his expression was friendly enough, she tried to read deeper, determine whether or not he was glad to see her. She wished it wasn't so, but she was glad to see him.

"Lily is awfully quick. She's tough to keep up with sometimes."

"Can we sit with you?" the little girl asked.

Mallory should be getting used to Lily's direct, unfiltered comments and questions. Mostly she was except when it came to Caleb. "Lily, he might be saving those seats."

He shrugged. "Travis and Anderson are around here somewhere, but they can find their own seats."

"Cool." Lily took the seat beside his. "You snooze, you lose."

"I couldn't have said it better." He laughed. "How are you, Mallory?"

"Fine." She was normally fast, funny and pretty good with words. It was kind of a requirement for her job. But being around Caleb stole her wit and sucked the volume out of her vocabulary. "You?"

"Never better." He indicated the chair next to Lily. "Why don't you have a seat? If you let me have your tickets, I'll get your plates."

The chivalrous offer made it impossible to keep the stutter out of her heartbeat. "Oh, that's not necessary. I don't want to trouble you."

"No trouble."

"I'll go, too, Caleb. I can show you what Aunt Mallory likes best."

"Good idea." He held out his hand and Lily took it.

"All right, then. Thanks."

Mallory watched the two of them walk over to the food, Caleb's big hand holding the little one. He took three plates and handed one to the little girl. At Lily's direction, he spooned scrambled eggs, hash browns, bacon and finally pancakes with syrup onto each of the two plates, then supervised Lily. When she had everything, her niece carefully carried her plate back to the table while he brought the other two.

"Here you go." He set it in front of her. "I'll go grab silverware and napkins."

While she waited, Lily took a bite of her bacon strip. "This is good."

The food maybe, not so much the situation. It seemed as if every time she turned around Caleb was there and he was nice. Nice made her nervous because it could lead to feelings she didn't want. Nice could be dangerous, but at least Lily was between them.

"Here you go, ladies." He handed out forks and knives, then sat down.

"I'm kind of surprised to see you here," she said to him.

"What? You thought I was a heathen?"

"No. But you said on a ranch there are always chores to do, even on Sunday." Mallory took a bite of the eggs. "And sometimes you can't attend."

"There are things that have to be done every day, but others can be put off to give us free time for the important things. This fund-raiser is important enough for a cowboy to take a break."

Lily looked up at him. "Why do they call you a cowboy when you're a man?"

"Good question." He thought for a moment. "It's a name that's been around over a hundred years for men who herd cows."

"What else do you do?" Lily cut off a piece of pancake and stuffed it into her mouth.

"Take care of horses." He finished chewing. "We get up early to do that."

"Why?"

"Because they're hungry. And then we muck out the stalls," he explained.

"What's a stall? And how do you muck it?" the little girl asked.

"Well," he said thoughtfully, "every horse has a space in the barn separated by a sort of fence and it's covered with hay to make it soft and cozy. The hay gets dirty and we have to shovel it out, to clean up after them."

"How does it get dirty?"

Mallory grinned at him. "I can't wait to hear the answer to that, too."

"You're enjoying this way too much." But his blue eyes twinkled with amusement. He said to Lily, "Do you know what horse droppings are?"

She thought for a second, then said, "Poop."

"That's right."

The little girl wrinkled her nose. "In the Fourth of July parade one of the horses did it. Amelia's mom told us what it was and that it was all natural, but we just went 'ew.' Doesn't it gross you out?"

He laughed. "No. I'm used to it."

"I bet it stinks," she persisted.

"Maybe if you're a city slicker." He scooped up the last of his eggs, then chewed and swallowed.

"What's a city slicker?" Lily wanted to know.

Mallory met his gaze. "Surely you were ready for that one."

"Yeah." He looked at the little girl. "It's someone who's never been around cows and horses before."

"Like me," she said.

"Yeah."

While finishing her breakfast, Mallory listened to them talk. Lily asked questions that ran the gamut from *What do horses eat?* to *Does your butt get sore when you ride a horse?* To Caleb's credit, he answered every single one and his level of patience was impressive. Not once did he look the least bit annoyed. It was enough to make even the most guarded heart go all soft and gooey—and Mallory's heart was pretty guarded. Or at least, it had been up until then…

"You should bring her out to the ranch," he said.

"I'm sorry, what?"

"I want to ride a horse, Auntie Mal." Lily's little face was full of eager and earnest anticipation.

Mallory's attention apparently slipped when her heart went all mushy for a minute. "We'll see."

"That's what you always say when you don't want me to do something. You think I'll forget, but I promise I won't. Since we moved here I've been wanting to see the horses but you're always too busy."

"That's to be expected," Caleb said quietly. "Your aunt works and takes care of you, Lily. That doesn't leave a lot of time left over."

"I know. It's just—" She looked up. "Sorry, Aunt Mallory."

"It's okay, ladybug." Mallory gave her a quick hug. "Obviously this means a lot to you, so we'll just have to find the time to make it happen."

"How about today?" Caleb said.

Mallory hadn't expected that. "What?"

"After breakfast," he said. "Bring her to the ranch. I'd be happy to show her what I do."

"I want to know if the barn smells icky," Lily said enthusiastically.

Was this what a flood felt like? Mallory wondered. Because she had the sensation of being swept away without anything to grab on to and stop the momentum.

"I thought you had chores to catch up on," she said to Caleb.

"They'll keep." He grinned. "Rust Creek Falls is ranching country. You've been here over six months and haven't been to one. If that's not illegal, it should be."

"Please, Auntie Mal." The pleading on Lily's face was just too much to resist.

Finally she said, "If you're sure we won't be a bother."

"I'm sure."

Caleb was sure, all right. Sure that he needed his head examined.

No one had been holding a gun, ordering him to invite

Mallory and Lily to the ranch. The idea had just popped into his mind and next thing he knew the words were coming out of his mouth.

Now they were here.

He watched the woman and child walk toward him after parking the car by his truck near the one-story ranch-style house where his brother Anderson lived. Mallory had stopped to change from her feminine, floral cotton dress into jeans and sneakers. Caleb couldn't decide which look he liked best, not even if there was a gun to his head. Way ahead of her aunt, Lily was wearing jeans now, too, and had on a pink baseball hat. She looked cute as could be.

"Hi." He was leaning against the hitching post in front of the house.

Lily was practically quivering with excitement. "Caleb, there's nothing around here but empty land!"

"That's sort of the point. On a ranch we raise big animals and they need a lot of room."

He was looking at the little girl but knew the exact moment Mallory caught up to her. She smelled like lemon, roses and sunshine. His reputation with women was no secret and it followed that he was something of an expert, at least in rating the scent of a female's skin. He was pretty sure that in a pitch-dark room full of women where he couldn't see his hand in front of his face, he would know Mallory was there and find his way to her. He was also pretty sure he'd never waxed that poetic about the scent of a woman before.

He lifted his gaze to hers and felt a confusing twist in his gut. She just looked so darn pretty with her auburn hair pulled into a ponytail and sunglasses pushed to the top of her head. She was small and curvy and smelled great, a triple threat as far as he was concerned. Watching his back seemed like an excellent idea.

"Did you have any trouble finding the place?" he asked.

"No. Your directions were good. And as Lily said, there wasn't a whole lot around to confuse me."

Lily grabbed his hand. "Show me the barn."

"Yes, ma'am." He grinned at her enthusiasm. "Are you always so bossy?"

"Aunt Mallory calls it determination."

"Good for Aunt Mallory," he said. "I bet you're always right."

"Not so much." Mallory watched her niece run ahead of them toward the barn, then called out, "Wait for Caleb. Don't go inside."

Caleb couldn't read her expression because she'd pulled her sunglasses down over her eyes. "Are you upset that she said you're always too busy?"

"Yes and no."

"Okay." That was sufficiently confusing. "It's okay if you don't want to talk about it."

"Oh, no. That's not what I meant." She put her hand on his arm.

The warm softness of her fingers nearly distracted him enough to keep him from asking what she did mean, but he pulled himself together. "Care to explain?"

"Yes, it bothers me that she thinks I'm too busy. But the fact that she verbalized it is a very big deal."

"Why?"

"Since I became her guardian, her response to things that upset her is measured, which means there's no push-back. As if she's afraid to be herself."

"Why would she be?"

"In counseling I learned a lot about what to watch for." She took a deep breath. "When her parents died, her safe world changed. She came to live with me but we'd only seen each other a handful of times and I was a virtual stranger. She's a smart kid. She knows you can return a puppy if it doesn't fit into the family. What if she made waves, popped off about being told no? What if I decided I didn't want her?"

"You wouldn't." There was no explaining why he was so sure, but he knew that as surely as he knew his last name was Dalton.

"Of course I wouldn't. I love her so much. And I think—I hope—she knows that. But devastating loss happened once, which in her mind opens up the possibility that it could again. I think she feels that expressing her discontent could make her world change again. So most of the time she's *too* good, if that makes any sense. But today she behaved like a normal kid." Mallory grinned at the memory. "She let me know how much this trip to the ranch means to her and that it's inconvenient for her that I have obligations. I was really happy she did that."

"Is that why you agreed to bring her here today?"

"Partly," she admitted.

"What's the other part?"

At that moment, Lily came running up to them. "You two are slowpokes. Hurry up. I've been waiting *forever* to go in the barn."

Although Caleb really wanted to know what else had factored into her decision to take him up on the invitation, he knew the moment to find out was gone.

"Okay," he said to the little girl. "I'm hurrying."

He opened one of the big barn doors and led them inside. "So, does it smell icky?"

Lily sniffed. "Yes."

"That's because you're a city slicker." He met the serious dark-eyed gaze and said, "But stick with me, kid. We'll fix that."

In front of them was a long, packed-dirt corridor with stalls on either side, several of them containing horses. The scene was as familiar to him as the face he saw in the mirror every day when he shaved, but this was a chance to see it with fresh eyes.

Lily's voice was barely a whisper when she asked reverently, "Is there a horse in every single space?"

"No." As they moved into the shady interior, the sound of whinnying and the stamp of hooves greeted him. "Hear that? They're telling me hello."

"Really? They know you?"

"Sure do."

"Where are the rest of the horses?" Mallory asked.

"Working." Confusion in their eyes made him explain. "We have a couple of cowboys on the payroll and they're out checking fences and cattle."

"Don't cattle just kind of hang out and graze?"

"They do. But stuff happens. Some of them are pregnant and that needs supervision in case there's a problem. It needs to be done several times a night, seven days a week."

"So the cattle don't recognize federal or religious holidays?" Mallory's voice was teasing.

"Nope. And if someone has the flu, they're completely unsympathetic."

"This job isn't for sissies." The words were teasing but there was respect in her tone.

"When you're raised to this life like my brothers and I were, it's just what is. I can't imagine doing anything else."

"I can imagine riding," Lily said.

He looked at Mallory. "Did you know you're raising a smart aleck there?"

"Key word being *smart*," she said.

"If it's all right with your aunt," he said to the little girl, "I'll pick out a horse for you and saddle him up."

Mallory's expression revealed that protective instinct was battling with her longing to give this child whatever she wanted. She was weighing risk and reward, like any mother would. "Is it dangerous?"

"I've got a horse in mind who's gentle and sweet. And I'll be right there the whole time." He pushed the brim of his hat up a notch and looked at Lily. "But it's important to always follow directions and pay attention to what you're doing."

"Why?" Lily asked.

"Because the animal is always thinking, just like you are. If you're distracted and don't outthink him, that's when you can get hurt."

"I promise to outthink him," she vowed.

"What do you say?" he asked Mallory.

"All right. But be careful," she warned.

"I will."

Caleb showed them around the barn first. The tack and supply rooms and where the tools were stored. He picked out a saddle and bridle, then went to the stall where the horse patiently waited.

"This is Shorty," he said, opening the gate.

Mallory checked out the pinto, who was only a little taller than her. "He is small."

Caleb heard the note of relief in her voice before he went inside and patted the horse's neck. "Hey, Shorty. You've got visitors."

The animal lifted his head slightly, then brought it down as if he was nodding agreement. "That's a good boy," Caleb crooned.

After sliding the bit into his mouth and securing it, he settled the blanket and saddle on the horse's back. He checked that the cinch wasn't too loose or too tight, then led the animal outside to the corral.

"Can I touch him?" Lily asked.

"You bet."

Caleb took her small hand and showed her how, letting her get used to the feel. When she was ready, he lifted her into the saddle.

"But I wanted to do it myself," she protested. "I didn't get to put my foot in that thing—"

"The stirrup."

"Yeah."

"Next time I'll get the step stool out."

"Why? He's small. I don't need it."

"You do, honey. Even I do sometimes."

"But you're big," she said, stating the obvious.

"Sometimes the horse is so big that to get my boot in the stirrup, I'd have to pull the saddle sideways. That would hurt him."

"I wouldn't want to do that." Lily looked subdued.

"Of course not. I know you wouldn't." He squeezed her shoulder, then took her hands and set them on the saddle horn. "Hold on to that. Grip his sides with your legs so you don't slide sideways. Get the feel of being in the saddle with the horse moving slowly."

"Okay."

Caleb led the horse slowly around the enclosure and frequently glanced over his shoulder to watch Lily, making sure she was relaxed and comfortable.

"This is fun," Lily said.

"You have to grip his sides," he reminded her. "Remember to pay attention. Outthink him."

"Okay."

Caleb sensed that Mallory was holding her breath as she watched them move around the corral, over and over, for about ten minutes. When Lily started to chatter, Caleb knew her attention and concentration were fading. He was about to change things up when he heard the saddle creaking behind him. About the same time Mallory gasped, Lily squealed and there was a plopping sound that told him she'd slid off and hit the ground.

Instantly he dropped the reins and Shorty stopped as

he'd been trained. Caleb went down on one knee beside the little girl, who'd started to cry.

"Lily!" Mallory ran over and knelt beside them. "Are you okay?"

"Does it hurt anywhere, Lily?" Caleb didn't think so. She'd fallen on her butt, which was good, since it had the most padding. But he checked out her arms and legs. There didn't seem to be anything wrong. Most likely she was just startled.

"Talk to me, honey," he coaxed the whimpering child.

"No, nothing hurts." She sniffled.

"Thank goodness." Mallory put a shaking hand to her chest. "I think it's time to get you home."

Caleb knew it wasn't a good idea to end her first horseback ride on a negative note. "I can't tell you what to do," he said. "But the thing is, anyone who wants to ride a horse needs to know that sooner or later you're going to fall off. The risk is implied."

Her mouth curved up slightly. "Spoken like the son of a lawyer."

"There's no escaping DNA." Then he turned serious again. "Getting back on the horse is a cliché, but the psychology is sound. After a mishap, the longer you wait to do what scares you, the bigger that thing becomes in your head. It's best to get right back on the horse and not let the challenge win."

"I don't know. What if—"

"Please, Auntie Mal. I promise I'll outthink him this time."

Mallory shook her head slightly, but said, "All right."

Caleb lifted Lily back into the saddle and within minutes the little girl relaxed. A half hour later you'd never know she fell. She was having a great time, as if she'd been born to the saddle.

Mallory had relaxed, too, smiling at him as if he'd done

something remarkable. The expression in her brown eyes made him feel like a hero, and the devil of it was that was a look he could get used to.

But getting in the habit of enjoying that look from a woman wasn't something he was anxious to do. He was single and liked it that way. Habits could be broken, but a man had better be sure he really wanted to, because life would never be the same, and not necessarily in a good way.

Chapter Five

Mallory walked into the Community Center, where folding metal chairs had been set up for Winona Cobbs's psychic lecture. Sally at Bee's Beauty Parlor had been right about almost everyone in town being there, not that Mallory was counting heads, but it looked like standing room only. She ended up standing in the back and could barely even see the stage, let alone an empty chair. So much for being early in order to find a good seat.

It was getting a little claustrophobic. Her statuesque friends didn't understand, but when you were five feet two inches tall, crowds closed in and people ran into you.

As if to prove the validity of that thought, a big man in front of her backed up and stepped on her foot.

He glanced over his shoulder. "Sorry. Didn't see you there."

"It's okay," she said automatically. She was used to it.

"Are you by yourself?" he asked.

"Yes." Mallory had dropped Lily off at a friend's house

and was really glad. The only thing worse than getting stepped on herself would be worrying about the little girl being crushed.

The man pointed to a place she couldn't see. "There's one chair in the third row from the front."

"That's all right. This is—"

But he was already stepping aside and urging her forward. "Grab it before someone else gets it."

"Thanks."

Mallory kept forgetting this was Rust Creek Falls, where folks looked out for one another. Staying in the back would have made it easy to slip out early without drawing attention, but she couldn't refuse the polite gesture.

The chairs were arranged in two groups with an aisle between. When the crowd parted and the view wasn't blocked, she saw the empty place and made her way to it. In the row just behind it, she saw fellow members of the Newcomers Club—Cecelia Clifton, Jordyn Cates, Vanessa Brent and Julie Smith. Callie Kennedy was on the end with her new fiancé, Nathan Crawford.

Mallory smiled and waved as she passed them, then moved forward. The man on the end had long legs and she couldn't get to the seat beside his without asking him to stand.

"Excuse me," she said. "Is anyone sitting there?"

Caleb looked up at her and did a double take. "Hey."

"Hi." Her heart did a happy little dance. Probably for that reason she felt the need to explain she wasn't stalking him. "Someone in the back pointed out this seat. I didn't know you were here."

"Should I be flattered or insulted?" His eyes crinkled in that charming way they did when he smiled.

"Hmm." She tapped her lip. "Probably you shouldn't take it any way at all because it's just the truth."

"Okay, then. I'm not saving this seat. But—" he stood

and looked down at her "—if I was flirting, I'd say I was saving it for the prettiest lady in Rust Creek Falls."

"How's that line working for you?" she teased.

"You tell me." He moved a little to let her get by.

Mallory did her best to keep her body from brushing against his, but it couldn't be helped because the space was so small. She did her best to be sorry about touching him, but couldn't manage that, either.

He bent closer and his voice was husky when he said, "I meant every word."

There wasn't a single cell in her body not quivering from the tone, the words, the contact. She just hoped the blush on her cheeks wasn't obvious when she said, "Thanks."

After sitting and settling her purse on the linoleum floor, she felt a tap on her right shoulder and turned. Cecelia Clifton gave her a thumbs-up. Her friend had long brown hair, brown eyes and an approving grin on her pretty face.

She leaned close and whispered, "How long have you and Caleb been dating?"

"We're not." She glanced at him, talking to someone across the aisle and not paying attention to the conversation beside him. "This was the only seat available."

"Right." Vanessa Brent, a tall, pretty brunette, gave her a wink. "We believe that."

"It's the truth," she protested. Lowering her voice, she added, "We're not dating."

"So, when you went out to see his ranch yesterday, that was just—" blonde Julie Smith searched for the right word "—not dating?"

"Yes." Mallory shrugged. "Lily was asking a lot of questions about what cowboys do and he invited us—both of us—to see the ranch."

"And what do cowboys do?" Jordyn Cates had blonde hair and a suggestive expression in her blue eyes.

"Oh, please." Mallory half turned and made a shushing gesture to her friends.

"We'll talk later," Cecelia said.

Caleb was looking at her when she faced front again. "What's up?"

"The Newcomers Club." She shrugged. "Part of the Rust Creek Falls gal rush."

"Ah." He grinned, obviously remembering her mocking the name commonly given to the recent influx of women.

She looked around the room. "I heard it would be crowded tonight, but didn't expect this."

"Winona Cobbs is kind of a legend. She's been around as long as I can remember. My parents, too."

"How old is she?"

"No one knows for sure. Best guess is somewhere in her nineties."

"Someone else told me the same thing." Their thighs touched and the resulting heat caused a momentary interruption in the flow of information from her brain to her mouth. "So, um, why did you come tonight? Are you getting in touch with your inner psychic?"

His mouth curved into a smile. "Yeah. I'm hoping to psychically connect with the cattle. That will make my job a lot easier."

"You could be a reality star. The cattle whisperer." She laughed. "No, seriously. Why?"

"My mother said that a woman of Winona's advancing age and experience is deserving of everyone's respect and the least we could do is show up and support her."

"Really?" She stared at him skeptically. "Your mother made you?"

"She simply pointed out that it was the polite thing to do." The charmingly roguish expression was replaced by an angelic one.

"You're afraid of her."

"Of course. I'm not an idiot."

"Big, strong man like you is afraid of his mother." He didn't seem the least bit uncomfortable about that revelation. For some reason she found that completely appealing and liked him all the more for it. And she already liked him quite a bit.

"Good evening, ladies and gentlemen." A lady from the Women's Auxiliary had approached the lectern, and the microphone amplified her voice, efficiently cutting off conversation. "To most of you our speaker tonight needs no introduction. But for those of you new to Rust Creek Falls, I'll give you a little background."

Mallory heard about the lecturer's early years in Whitehorn, Montana, where she owned The Stop 'n Swap, or as she liked to call it, an edgy antiques store. Folks were skeptical of her sensitivity to nonphysical forces, but more often than not found her premonitions, situational insights and astral projections not only helpful, but right on the money. In other words, Winona Cobbs knew things she had no business knowing. Currently she wrote a syndicated blog called *Wisdom by Winona*.

"Tonight," the woman finished, "the Women's Auxiliary of Rust Creek Falls is pleased to welcome Winona Cobbs, who will give us pointers on how to get in touch with our own inner psychic."

As the room erupted in applause, Caleb leaned over and whispered, "When this is over, I expect to be able to read your mind."

Mallory's eyes widened at his suggestive expression and she was awfully grateful that he didn't know her thoughts right that moment. Because she wanted very much for him to kiss her.

A stoop-shouldered, silver-haired woman walked to the lectern. Even from the third row it was impossible to tell what color her eyes were, but the intelligence, vibrancy and life jumped out when she smiled.

"There are many psychic abilities," she said, getting right down to business. "Apportation—teleportation of an object. Bilocation—being in multiple places. Claircognizance—the ability to discern a psychic past, present or future from an individual. Precognition—knowing something in advance of its occurrence."

Caleb and Mallory looked at each other. She didn't know about him, but her head was ready to explode. Hopefully, there wasn't a quiz later.

"Any happening that can't be rationally explained goes under the heading of psychic and given a fancy name. I can see your eyes glazing over." Winona paused and looked at her audience, then smiled. "But I'm going to focus on two and give you some pointers for developing the skill in yourself. Studies have been done that indicate most people only use ten percent of their brain. We all are capable of psychic ability and simply need to stretch those muscles. So to speak.

"First, mediumship, which is channeling or communicating with spirits. All of us either have or will in the future lose someone in our lifetime that we're close to. Remember that love is very powerful. You can't see it or hold it in your hand, but it's eternal. It never dies. We want to know that the person we love who is gone is okay. And they want to know we are."

Mallory realized that was very true. Her sister was gone and she, Mallory, had so many questions. Had Mona been scared when the accident happened? They'd said she and her husband died instantly, but how could anyone know for sure? Was Mona really in a better place? Happy and content? Could she see that Mallory was doing her best to care for the child she'd left behind? Raise her the way Mona and Bill would have wanted?

As the questions hummed through her mind, she felt a big, warm hand on hers. She looked up at Caleb. There was sympathy and understanding in his eyes. It was an expression that said he knew what she was thinking and she shouldn't feel alone. She opened her tight fist and linked her fingers with his, which at that moment seemed more important than listening. A feeling of contentment settled over her and somehow she knew her sister was all right and approved of her taking care of Lily.

"The next ability I want to talk about is precognition. Prediction of events before they happen." Winona rested her hands on the lectern and looked out over it. "It's different from seeing the future and not that difficult. For example…a child is running through the house when you have told them to stop multiple times. Those are the ones who go to the school of hard knocks and give their parents gray hair." She paused as people laughed. "So this child is running and then falls. The first words out of your mouth are *I told you that would happen.*" A buzz went through the audience and heads were nodding, indicating everyone could relate. "My advice is this. Don't ignore your gut instinct. Pay attention to the signs that the universe is sending out."

Winona Cobbs talked awhile longer but Mallory was too distracted by how good Caleb's hand felt still holding hers to absorb much of anything that was said. Until the very end.

"I know we'd all like the message spelled out neat and tidy. A big sign in bold black letters that says *Pay attention now because this person is going to be important.*" Winona was looking straight at Mallory when she said, "Have you ever had someone come into your life who could have crossed your path many times before but didn't? Then suddenly they keep turning up wherever you are? Like a piece of lint you can't get rid of? Coincidence? Signs from the universe? Or a subconscious desire creating a powerful force that draws you both together? By embracing your inner psychic, you can find the answers."

The applause was enthusiastic and after the announcement was made about refreshments, everyone stood to leave. Caleb was still holding her hand and it felt right, too right. Although Mallory could almost feel the people around them staring. She wanted to explain that they were friends, nothing more, and she hoped no one got the wrong idea.

Mayor Collin Traub and his wife, Willa Christensen Traub, were across the aisle with knowing smiles on their faces. Finally the dark-haired, reformed bad boy said to them, "When did you two start dating?"

She and Caleb looked at each other and said together, "We're not dating."

"Uh-huh." That skeptical comment came from behind her and sounded a lot like Callie.

Mallory looked over her shoulder at the other Newcomers Club member. "Seriously, we just met."

"Oh?" Callie's eyebrow lifted as she looked up at the man she was engaged to. "Like Winona just said, what was that again, Nate?"

He said, "Something about someone who just crossed your path being important in your life. Paying attention to signs."

"Well," Caleb said, "this is nothing like that."

"You act as if *date* is a dirty word," the other man said.

Caleb saw a break in the flow of exiting people and stepped into the aisle, backing up a step so Mallory could precede him. She did and hurried out before anyone else could accuse them of dating.

They walked outside, where tables were set up with coffee, water, punch and a potluck of desserts. The area was illuminated by spotlights mounted on the corners of the Community Center. Side by side she and Caleb browsed the goodies. After looking at everything, she took a chocolate-chip cookie and a brownie, then some punch. He did the same. *Coincidence?* she wondered. This was just too woo-woo weird.

Moving away from the tables, where a lot of the crowd had congregated, they wandered over the grass and stopped a little off to themselves while other people milled around nearby.

Thoughtfully, Mallory nibbled on the cookie. After swallowing, she asked, "Do you think I should have a T-shirt made that says *I'm not dating Caleb Dalton?*"

"Maybe." He laughed. "But folks in Rust Creek Falls are going to think what they want no matter what we say. Even if we did put it on a sign."

"You've lived here longer and probably know that better than me. I suppose it only matters that we know the truth."

"I suppose."

But she would swear he was looking at her mouth with a dark intensity that made her nervous, in a sexy way. *Keep talking,* she told herself. "So, what did you think of the lecture?"

"Color me skeptical." He'd finished his brownie and only had half the cookie left. "I'm one of those guys who have to see it, touch it, before deciding something is the real deal."

"So, you don't believe in signs from the universe?"

"Not so much." He'd finished his cookie and drink and tossed the paper cup into the trash can nearby. "Can I take yours?"

Mallory handed him her empty napkin and cup and he disposed of them. "Thanks.

"No problem. What did you think?"

"I can't argue with the word *skeptical.*" She folded her arms over her chest. "If I had any inner psychic to embrace,

I'd never have gotten involved with the man who dumped me because I didn't make time for him."

"You mind explaining that?"

Darn it, she thought. She'd hardly intended to cry about her breakup on Caleb's shoulder. She sighed. "His name was Dustin and he was a resident at the hospital in Helena. I worked as a paralegal for a law firm. Granted, my job wasn't life-and-death like his, but it's still important. He worked much longer hours than I did, but when I put him off because of work one too many times, he broke things off."

"And broke your heart." He wasn't asking a question.

"I went through all the stages of grief—anger, denial, plotting revenge."

"I don't think I ever heard that getting even is one of those steps," he commented, his mouth curving up in a smile.

She laughed. "Probably ending it was for the best. Clearly he's self-centered and demanding. When I became Lily's guardian it probably would have ended anyway. But if she'd come into my life when we were a couple and then he walked out, that would have been one more adjustment for her to make."

"Sounds like the guy is a jerk," he said.

Talking about her past made her remember the first six months with her niece and how different their life was here in Rust Creek Falls. "What do you think about gut instinct?"

"I like to think of it more as flying by the seat of my pants. Spontaneous. Seems to work out."

"Hmm," she said. "I've always been a planner. Decisions were always made with a lot of thought and a long list of pros and cons. Until Rust Creek Falls."

"How so?" He slid his fingertips into the pockets of his jeans.

"I decided to move here and it was purely a gut-instinct

choice. I read Lissa's blog and suddenly missed Montana. New York was hectic and sad, and moving seemed really right."

"Do you still feel that way?"

"Yes. I can't think of a single time that I regretted it."

She laughed. "Lily missed the city and all the conveniences of take-out food and entertainment choices, but now I think she's pretty well-adjusted." She looked up and he had that hungry expression on his face again. "It seems she's in love with horses and riding. I'm not sure whether to curse you or be grateful."

He laughed. "So she enjoyed it."

"Very much. I appreciate you taking the time with her."

"It was fun. I'd be happy to teach you how to ride, too."

Mallory was trying to think of a diplomatic way to turn him down when she noticed Winona Cobbs. The woman walked by them mumbling something that sounded like, "I know I saw something. Could it be…"

She stopped a few feet away and stood there, looking around. Oblivious to the crowd.

Mallory glanced from the old woman to Caleb. "Do you think she's all right?"

"Define 'all right.' She just talked to the whole town about signs from the universe," he said.

"Still…" She twisted her fingers together. "I think I'm going to talk to her."

Before she could, Winona turned, shaking her head. She walked over to them and said to Caleb, "You think I'm a crazy old woman."

"No, ma'am." There was just the slightest tinge of guilt in his tone.

"A white lie is a lie nonetheless." But there was a twinkle in her eyes. Then it disappeared. "I thought I saw something. Someone. But now it's gone."

"So, your Spidey sense was tingling?" Caleb asked.

"Didn't your mother ever teach you that no one likes a smart aleck, Caleb Dalton?" Winona smiled. "I know you're a doubter, but that's all right. Still, if you don't believe anything else, believe this. It's never wise to ignore signs from the universe."

"I'll keep that in mind," he said.

Winona looked at him as if she could see something that no one else could. "He has his flaws, Mallory, but there's a good and true heart in there."

Mallory had a million questions, not the least of which was how the woman knew her name. But before she could ask anything, Winona walked away.

"How did she do that?"

"What?" he asked.

"I've never met her. She knew my name." She held her arms out helplessly.

"Really?" Wonder widened his eyes. "Maybe someone pointed you out and told her."

"I guess. That would explain it." She looked up at him and was glad he couldn't read her mind because right at that moment she wished he would kiss her. The irony of that after denying to her friends that they were dating didn't escape her. It was time to go. "This has been really fun, Caleb, but it's getting late and I have to pick Lily up at her friend's house."

"Right. I'll walk you to your car."

"That's nice of you." *Although not necessary,* she thought. After all, this was Rust Creek Falls.

Side by side they walked around the building to the Community Center parking lot. Her car was in a row farthest from the building and there was no one around. Mallory hit the button on the key fob and unlocked it, then Caleb opened the door.

She tossed her purse on the passenger seat and looked up. "I had a good time."

"Me, too."

And that was when Mallory got her second surprise of the evening. Caleb moved closer, bent slightly at the waist and pulled her against him. His mouth lowered to hers, warm and soft. Her hands slid over his chest, tangling around his neck as he nibbled kisses over her lips. The touch sent heat pouring through her and it pooled in her belly.

Her breath caught and then came faster. Caleb's breathing was none too steady, either. As kisses went, it was the best one she'd ever had and that opinion had nothing to do with the fact that she hadn't been kissed in a very long time.

His mouth was a whisper away from hers. "I can hear you thinking."

"Watch it. Your inner psychic is acting up."

His mouth curved up in a sexy smile. "Wouldn't be the first time."

"Speaking of which…" She dragged in air and reluctantly stepped away from the warmth of his body and the security of his arms. "What was that?"

"Define 'that.'"

"Kissing me."

"Ah." He blew out a breath. "It was me getting into my surroundings."

It could be that the kiss had her brain malfunctioning, but she didn't get what he meant. "I'm sorry. I need a little more than that."

"All night we've been hearing about gut instinct and looking for signs. For example," he said, "the last seat in the Community Center was next to mine and you took it. Was that a sign?"

"Now you're talking crazy and it's starting to scare me," she teased. "But for the sake of argument—a sign of what?"

"That I should kiss you. I decided to see what would happen if I didn't ignore it and followed my gut instinct."

"And?"

"It wasn't wrong." He grinned. "You're a really good kisser, Mallory Franklin. It was every bit as nice as I thought it would be. And—"

"What?" Her voice was one part breathless and one part anticipation.

"I'm thinking signs again." He folded his arms over his chest. "Maybe it means you should go out with me. After all, it's not a good idea to thumb your nose at signs from the universe."

"Hmm." Mallory nodded. "I see what you mean."

"Is that you saying yes?"

"It is."

That affirmative answer came from gut instinct but Mallory couldn't help it. She liked the prospect of a night of fun with a cute cowboy and the thought was irresistible.

Who said it had to mean anything?

Chapter Six

The day after learning to embrace his inner psychic, Caleb picked Mallory up at her house. He could have waited until the weekend, but when the universe hands out signs, you don't look the other way. And he was glad he hadn't. He'd had such a good time with her last night, all day he'd been looking forward to seeing her again.

After saying good-night to Lily and Cecelia Clifton, who was babysitting, he walked Mallory to his truck parked at the curb. He opened the door for her. "This was really short notice. I'm glad you didn't have plans."

"It's fate. I happened to have an opening in my busy social calendar." Before putting a foot on the running board to climb into the truck, she gave him a wry look. "There's nothing on my schedule these days except work and spending time with Lily."

He made sure she was settled before closing the door, then walked around to climb into the driver's seat. "Then I'm glad Cecelia was free to stay with her."

"Me, too. So where are we going?"

Caleb met her gaze and thought she was as pretty as a picture sitting there beside him. For a second or two the sight of her took his breath away. Excitement was shining in her eyes and hummed in her voice and for a moment he couldn't think straight, let alone answer.

Finally he said, "Don't you want to be surprised?"

"For someone who doesn't make a move without some serious strategic planning, that's a loaded question."

"And yet you moved to Rust Creek based solely on instinct and it worked out. That tells me you need more surprises in your life and you'll find out when we get there."

"Okay."

It sounded as if she trusted him, and he liked that a lot.

The Ace in the Hole wasn't far, so the suspense didn't last very long. He drove into the parking lot that even on a weeknight had a good number of trucks, which made sense, since it was a favorite hangout for local cowboys. Tonight there were also a few motorcycles and cars.

"I've been in Rust Creek Falls for over six months and lately I seem to be broadening my horizons. I've never been here," she said.

Caleb was happier about that than he had any business being, but he didn't like the idea of her coming here alone. The clientele leaned toward young, single, rowdy guys who were looking to let off steam.

"The food is pretty good," he said. "I thought we could have dinner and get to know each other."

"Sounds good." She smiled, then opened her door and slid out of the truck.

Just ahead they could see the old-fashioned hitching post out front to tie horses for cowboys who rode them into town. Lighted beer signs in the window left no doubt about what kind of establishment was inside, and over the door an oversize playing card, an ace of hearts, blinked in red neon. Caleb walked beside Mallory, close enough that the skirt of her summer cotton dress brushed his jeans. Her short-sleeved yellow sweater seemed to wrap her in sunshine.

Caleb opened the screen door with the rusty hinges and winced at the screech that seemed to contrast with her fresh innocence—and not in a good way. He tried to see the place through her eyes. To the right there was a scarred bar with stools in front that ran the length of the wall. A mirror behind it reflected the bottles of liquor lined up there. Booths ringed the outer wall and circular tables big enough for six, or however many chairs could be pulled up, surrounded the dance floor in the middle of the room. The antique Wurlitzer jukebox was playing a country song and in the far back corner men were playing darts and pool.

The rest of the cowboys in the place stared openly at Mallory the second she walked in. With his hand at the small of her back, he felt the exact moment she noticed the male attention and tensed up.

"Do we have to wait to be seated?" she whispered.

"No." He chuckled. "It's not that kind of place." He urged her toward a booth, which offered more privacy than the tables. Unfortunately the guys and a group of women sitting at the tables could still check them out.

On top of that, it suddenly hit him that she'd lived in New York. The wait-to-be-seated question was a big clue about her once-sophisticated life.

They sat across from each other on the padded faux-leather seats. Caleb met her gaze. "So, this must be different for you."

"My friends in the Newcomers Club have talked about coming here for girls' night." That didn't really answer the question. "They left out a lot of details."

"It has local color."

"Uh-huh." Mallory's eyes widened as she glanced around, then quickly looked back at him.

Caleb noticed Lani behind the bar. She worked here part-time and was talking to her boss. He knew his little sister could handle herself if some dude got out of line, but it was a comfort that the owner's new husband spent a lot of time here in the evening with his wife. Sam Traven was a retired navy SEAL and could deal with a drunken cowboy with one hand tied behind his back.

When Rosey Shaw Traven headed their way, Caleb again tried to see her through Mallory's eyes. The woman was in her mid-sixties and wore a peasant blouse, leather vest and wide belt over her tight jeans. She had dark hair, brown eyes and still flirted with the men and flaunted her assets. He wasn't sure whether or not to be relieved that she would be their waitress instead of his sister.

"Hey, handsome." She looked away from him to Mallory. "You're new in town. Do I need to warn you about this good-looking rascal?"

That was when Caleb made up his mind to not be relieved about Rosey. At least Lani had Sunday dinner with Mallory and would have been friendly but not outrageous. Rosey knew most of his secrets and didn't mind telling anyone who would listen.

"I'd appreciate a warning very much." She smiled and extended her hand. "Mallory Franklin."

"Rosey Traven." She shook hands, then said, "Pleased to meet you."

Before the secret sharing could commence, Caleb said, "Can we get a couple of menus?"

"Really? You bring a different girl in here every night. How come you don't know it by heart?" Rosey shook a finger at him. "And don't tell me it's because of how often it changes. I've only added salads and wraps to accommodate all the ladies from the Rust Creek Falls gal rush."

"You know Mallory isn't part of that," he said quickly.

Rosey took her measure. "Don't say."

"What he means is that I didn't come here looking for a man."

"Maybe not, but—" she angled her head toward the tables in the center of the room "—they're sure looking at you."

"I noticed."

And Caleb noticed that the excitement was missing from her voice now, and that bothered him. He'd let her down and didn't like that he had.

"So, I'll go get those menus." Rosey started to turn away.

"That's okay," Mallory said quickly. "I'll have a burger."

"Make it two." Caleb just needed a little time to turn this around.

He'd been told by more than one woman that he was charming, and now was the time to turn up the power. When the bar owner walked away, he smiled. "So, this must be really different from your life in New York."

Her attention shifted from the men still checking her out and back to him. "That's the second time you mentioned that I'm not from around here."

"It's a conversation starter." He gave her the grin that was guaranteed to put a lady in a good mood.

Her lips curved up. "As you already know, I'm originally from Montana, so this isn't like stepping off a spaceship onto the surface of Mars. New York is where I really felt out of place."

When the rusty screen door opened, he looked over and saw Sharla Jenkins walk in. She was blonde, built and looking for action. Caleb knew that because he'd taken her up on the offer once upon a time, but once was all it would ever be and they both knew that. Still, when she spotted him, a smile spread across her pretty face and she headed his way.

"Caleb Dalton, you handsome devil. How are you?" Before he could answer, she looked at Mallory. "I haven't seen you in here before. Must be new in town."

"Six months now. I'm Mallory Franklin."

"Sharla Jenkins." She winked at Caleb. "Don't let this big bad cowboy break your heart like he did mine."

It was hard to maintain a level of charm when you were really annoyed. "That's not true."

"Mallory knows I'm teasing."

The pinched expression on the lady's face made him pretty sure she didn't know that at all. "You and I are just friends."

"*Good* friends, if you know what I mean," she said to Mallory.

"You're probably meeting someone here." This would go from bad to worse unless Caleb could move her along. "It's been nice seeing you, Sharla."

"You trying to get rid of me?"

"That would be my guess," Mallory said, her tone cool and cynical.

"A woman who's not afraid to stake her claim. I can respect that." Sharla smiled and nodded. "Okay, then. See you around."

She moved away and pulled up a chair with the other women at the table near the plank floor. When the music changed to George Strait's "I Cross My Heart," a cowboy walked over to her and held out his hand. Sharla took it and the two started moving around the dance floor.

Maybe he should ask Mallory. Dancing might turn things around and he sure would like an excuse to see what her sexy curves would feel like in his arms. He opened his mouth to suggest it when Lani walked over with a tray holding two longneck bottles of beer.

"Hi, Mallory. Nice to see you again." His sister gave him a look that said she wasn't surprised to see him here with this woman.

Mallory's smile was friendly. "How are you, Lani? I didn't know you worked here."

"I help out now and then." She put a bottle in front of each of them.

"We didn't order those," Mallory protested.

Lani pointed to the guy who hadn't taken his eyes off Mallory since they'd walked in the door. He had the nerve to tip his hat. "He sent it over."

Then she indicated a pretty brunette who waggled her fingers at Caleb. "She bought yours and asked me to give you her phone number." Lani put a cocktail napkin with numbers on it in front of him. "I had to do this because it's my job, but I'll return it to her if you want."

"Don't bother." Ignoring it would send a stronger message.

"Okay, then." She smiled at each of them. "Enjoy your evening."

"Right," he muttered, feeling like an idiot.

"I feel like I've been brought to school for show-and-tell." Mallory pulled that bright yellow sweater tighter, then folded her arms over her chest. It was possible for her to look more uncomfortable, but only if a pack of alligators were nipping at her toes.

Caleb could talk the ears off an elephant, but he had no idea what to say. The reality was clear—he felt like an idiot because he officially was one. It was time to admit defeat and get the hell out.

"Mallory, would you like to go?"

"More than you can possibly know."

He slid out of the booth and offered her his hand, which she ignored. That proved his point about failing to acknowledge a gesture sending a strong message. After tossing some bills on the table to pay Rosey for her trouble, he let Mallory precede him out the door and to the truck. She didn't say anything on the drive back to her place and couldn't get out fast enough after he turned off the ignition. For a small woman she sure could move and it was almost a challenge to keep up with her.

"Mallory, wait," he said when she reached for the handle on the front door. "Let's talk about this."

"Talking won't make it any less a disaster."

"At least let me apologize for taking you there on a first date." His father always said he was good with words and could have been a lawyer if he'd wanted. Caleb hoped that was true because he didn't want this to be the last date. "I'm asking you to trust me one more time. Give me a do-over."

"Not a good idea." She settled the strap of her purse more securely on her shoulder. "Maybe this is a sign that going out is a mistake. Consider yourself off the hook."

He knew how it felt to want off the hook and that was not how he was feeling now. The circumstances could have been better, but being with her didn't feel like a mistake. Before he could pull together an argument to make his case, the front door opened.

"I thought I heard voices out here." Pretty brunette Cecelia Clifton stood there with Lily beside her. They wore twin expressions of confusion. "You guys have barely been gone an hour."

"How come you're home so early, Auntie Mal?"

"It was time." Mallory opened her purse. "I'll pay you for the whole evening, Cece."

"No, you won't."

"It's hardly worth your time," Mallory disagreed.

"Are you kidding? I love hanging out with Lily. When you work as a construction assistant, it's all guys. We had some quality girl time." She looked down at the little girl. "Right, kiddo?"

"Yes."

Cecelia refused to take the bill Mallory tried to hand her and started toward her truck. "See you soon."

"We played dolls. Cecelia was going to show me how to French-braid hair." Lily's little face had the beginnings of a pout on it.

"Another time," her aunt said.

"The next time you go out with Caleb?" she asked hopefully.

Never let it be said that he missed an opportunity. "What a coincidence. We were just talking about that."

"There's nothing more to say."

"So, when are you going out with him?" Lily wanted to know.

"There's nothing specific," Mallory answered vaguely.

"We should nail it down." Caleb knew it was two against one but wasn't above using it to get what he wanted.

Mallory's eyes narrowed, telling him she knew exactly what he was doing and wouldn't play. "We'll talk about it later."

"Okay." He would hold her to that.

"Caleb, are you going to kiss Aunt Mallory goodnight?"

"No, he's not. And that's an inappropriate question, young lady."

"Why?" Lily was persistent. "That's what happens in the movies."

"This isn't a movie," her aunt said.

"No, it's not." Caleb remembered his father saying that sometimes a lawyer needed to know when to stop talking. It was good advice no matter what your profession and this was one of those times.

"Lily, it's time for you to get ready for bed."

"Okay, Aunt Mallory. 'Night, Caleb."

"Sleep tight, Lily."

"Wait, I have to tell you one more thing."

"What?" he asked, going down on one knee in front of her.

"I just wanted you to know. Travis isn't my favorite cowboy. You are." She threw her arms around his neck.

"I'm flattered. And you're my favorite little cowgirl."

When the little girl was gone, he moved close to Mallory, settling his hands on her arms before gently urging her against him. Then he lowered his mouth to hers. Last night's kiss had been about testing the waters, but now he was going to prove a point. He slid one arm around her waist, then threaded the fingers of his other hand through the silk of her pretty, dark red hair.

With the tip of his tongue he traced her lips, letting her know exactly what he would do if there wasn't an eight-year-old close by. He kept up gentle, nibbling kisses until he heard her soft sigh and knew that, for now, his work here was done.

Reluctantly he stepped away from her and saw the glazed, dazed expression in her eyes. She could pretend there wouldn't be a next time but her reaction to the kiss said different.

"Good night, Mallory." He backed away and walked to his truck.

He hadn't completely struck out tonight. Lily liked him.

At least he was someone's favorite. Mallory might think this was over, but he wasn't done yet. Not by a long shot.

Caleb had messed up with Mallory once and didn't want the second time around to be a repeat. So when chores on the ranch were finished the next day, he took a ride into town. The first stop was to see his dad. Ben Dalton was the wisest man Caleb had ever met and that opinion had nothing to do with the fact that they were related.

It was late in the afternoon when he parked his truck in the lot by his dad's law office and walked inside. This time Lily wasn't at the front desk and he greeted Jessica Evanson, the receptionist. She was blonde, blue-eyed and somewhere in her early to mid-twenties. He'd once thought about asking her out but decided not to since she worked for his dad. Maybe part of the reason he was here had to do with getting permission to cross that line.

"Hi," he said.

"Hey, Caleb. How are you?"

"Good. You?" He stopped at the desk.

"Great."

"Is my dad busy?"

She gave him a wry look. "Always."

"Let me rephrase. Is he with a client?"

"No. He's between appointments."

"Can I go back?"

"Sure. If he doesn't want to see you, he has no problem telling you."

"I've been thrown out of better places than this," he teased.

"And probably worse." She laughed. "I'll let him know you're on your way."

"Thanks."

Caleb walked through the doorway separating the reception and waiting areas from offices. He knew his father's was at the end of the hall and headed in that direction. The faint scent of perfume drifted to him and he knew it belonged to Mallory. His heart jerked as if he was standing on her front porch holding her, kissing her with everything he had. As far as he was concerned that was the only part of last night's dud of a date that had worked.

There were voices coming from her office, telling him

she was with someone, which was just as well. It was tempting to stop and say hi, but he didn't want to do that until after talking with his dad. So he forced himself to walk on by. Without looking in.

Outside his father's open door, he paused, then rapped his knuckles on the doorjamb. "Hey, Dad."

Ben looked up from the computer. "Caleb. Good to see you, son. Come in."

"Is this a bad time?" He moved to the desk.

"If you're asking whether or not I'm busy, the answer is yes. But it's nothing I can't put on hold for a few minutes." He grinned, then held out his hand, indicating the two club chairs in front of his desk. "Have a seat."

"Thanks."

"To what do I owe the honor of a visit from my number-three son?"

"Honor?"

"It's unexpected. Usually ranch legal work brings you in, but we already took care of that. So, if this has nothing to do with my pretty paralegal and your recent date with her, I'm at a loss to explain why you're here."

Caleb squirmed in the chair and felt like a twelve-year-old waiting for an ear blistering after some foolish prank. But to get to the advice part, he had to own up to the bone-headed move first.

"Did you hear anything about what happened?" he asked.

"No. But Mallory has been in a mood all day and that's not like her. What did you do?"

Besides kissing her good-night, a kiss that made him want her so bad he ached in places he never had before? Caleb met his father's shrewd gaze. "I took her to the Ace in the Hole for dinner."

A blank expression on his face, Ben leaned back in his chair, resting his hands on his flat stomach. There was some silver in his hair now and lines in his face, but he was still a handsome man. "I suppose if it had gone well you wouldn't be here now."

"True enough. Between women eyeing me like a prime piece of meat and ornery cowboys checking her out..." He removed his Stetson and dragged his fingers through his hair. "Then there was Sharla Jenkins, who made sure to stop by our table and say hello."

"One-night stand, I'm guessing."

"That's not really important, Dad." He shifted in his seat. "The point is, you're right. It didn't go very well with Mallory."

"Sorry to hear that, son." Ben shook his head sympathetically. "She's good people. Fate threw her a really lousy curve ball, and instead of whining and trying to dodge it, she's stepping up."

"Yeah." Caleb admired that about her, too.

"It wasn't her choice to adopt that little girl, but her sister did. And Mallory is picking up where she left off—making choices of her own."

Besides moving here and being a mother? "What is she doing?"

"Can't say," his dad said mysteriously. "Attorney-client privilege."

"So you're doing legal work for her?"

"Not the point."

"Then what is?"

"She's a good woman. Salt of the earth. The kind a man would be lucky to have walking beside him through life—"

"Dad—"

"Too much?" His father grinned.

"You and Mom aren't subtle about wanting all of us to settle down and have kids."

"Only if it's right." A serious expression replaced the

grin. "And that makes me wonder why you came to talk to me about Mallory."

"Is there a law against it?"

"Not that I'm aware of, but you never have before."

Because it never seemed as important before, Caleb realized. And he didn't want to think too much about why Mallory was different. She'd claimed to usually be a planner and that moving to Rust Creek Falls was the only decision she'd ever made purely on instinct.

Caleb was just the opposite—flying by the seat of his pants. But he'd done that in taking her to Ace in the Hole and look how that turned out. Now he was going to plan—with his dad's help.

"Look, Dad, I screwed up."

"You'll get no argument from me."

"Thanks for the support," he said wryly. "But here's the thing. I want to ask her out again, but I can't invite myself to her place for dinner."

"No, that would be rude and she might think you're hitting on her. Same thing if you ask her to your place. Actually, that would be worse, since Lily wouldn't be there for a chaperone." His dad thought for a moment. "You could extend a dinner invitation to them both, but I'm guessing you're after something more private, where the two of you can become better acquainted."

"Exactly." Leave it to his dad to put a finer point on the problem. "So, any suggestions?"

"Take her to Kalispell. It's bigger than Rust Creek, so not everyone knows you. Your mother and I go there from time to time."

"Somewhere special?"

"North Bay Grill is good. Romantic."

Anyplace they weren't on display like mackerels in an aquarium would be an improvement, but Caleb liked the sound of romantic.

"Rising Sun Bistro is also nice. Great food." There was a twinkle in his father's eyes. "Just an FYI, I'd steer clear of any establishment with the word *bar, saloon* or *pub* in the title."

"Yeah. I sort of figured that one out for myself. Okay, Dad. I'll get out of your hair. Thanks for the advice." He stood.

His father did the same and walked him to the door. "One more thing, son. And this is unsolicited counsel, but my gut is telling me to say it anyway."

"Okay."

"You're a grown man and last time I checked you were smart enough to figure out what went wrong and how to fix it." His father slid his hands into the pockets of the jeans he wore unless appearing before a court judge. "This visit was about securing my blessing to go out with a woman who is an employee of mine."

"And?" He wasn't surprised his dad had figured that out and didn't pretend to be.

"I've got mixed feelings," the older man admitted.

That did surprise Caleb. "I thought you liked her."

"I do. The thing is, your track record with women is impressive in volume but not so much when you're talking substance."

No one knew that better than Caleb. He was all about fun and no commitment. "Dad, I—"

Ben held up his hand. "There's nothing wrong with that as long as everyone involved is on the same page. Your mother and I have made it a point not to get attached to any young woman who catches your eye. Until now."

"With Mallory?"

"We're very fond of her," his father confirmed. "And we don't want her hurt."

"I wouldn't do that."

"You wouldn't *mean* to," Ben qualified. "Just keep in

mind that Mallory isn't your usual type. She's not a fast and loose kind of woman."

"Yes, sir. I'll do that." So he had provisional permission to ask his father's paralegal for another date.

The two of them stood their ground for several moments before shaking hands. Ben went back to his desk and Caleb paused outside his door. He waited for internal confirmation that Mallory wasn't his type and asking for a do-over was barking up the wrong tree. That was what usually happened, but this time there was only silence.

That was good enough for him. He liked her; they'd had fun last night on the drive to the Ace in the Hole. And the kiss was spectacular. More important, he wanted to see where this would go.

He really wanted to see whether or not the good times they'd shared were a fluke. If so, he would back off. No harm, no foul.

No one would get hurt.

Chapter Seven

Mallory had seen Caleb walk by her office and wondered what he was doing here. Scratch that. He'd come to see his father, but about what? Seemed too much of a coincidence, since their disastrous date was just the night before. That was disturbing enough, but it was more disconcerting how even a glimpse of him could skewer her concentration. She'd nearly sent Mr. and Mrs. Taylor on their way without signing all the paperwork for their trust. That was not normal for her and she didn't like it one bit.

Now she was at her desk buried in paperwork and trying to recover her focus. That was proving to be a challenge, since she didn't know whether or not he'd left the building. The man made her nervous. Not in a bad way, just in a she-couldn't-think-straight-when-he-was-in-the-same-room way.

It was probably for the best that last night's date had been a disaster, giving her an excuse to nip this whatever-it-was in the bud. In spite of his asking for another chance and even the most spectacular kiss she'd ever had, when the sun came up he almost surely had realized he was better off with Sharla Jenkins. Or someone else equally as uncomplicated and—dare she say it—stacked.

Looking down at her own less-than-impressive bosom, she sighed. "I'm sure men are more attracted to a woman's brains than her boobs."

"Who's a boob?" Jessica Evanson stood in her doorway.

"No one."

"Were you talking about Caleb? I heard you were out with him last night at the Ace in the Hole."

"That's true." She almost welcomed the change of subject in order to avoid any reference to or explanation of the boob remark.

"And?"

"What?" Mallory didn't like playing dumb when she wasn't, but that was preferable to talking about her boss's son. "You want details and there's nothing to tell."

"I can't believe Sharla had the nerve to talk to him while he was there with you."

Mallory wasn't used to being the subject of town talk. Since arriving in Rust Creek Falls, she'd flown under the radar, settling in and being a mother to Lily. That had changed when she agreed to a date with gossip magnet Caleb Dalton.

"Who told you all this?" she demanded, wondering how the information had spread so fast.

"Lani Dalton. We're friends. She said Caleb didn't look very happy when Sharla stopped by your table."

"He seemed friendly enough." A little too friendly as far as Mallory was concerned.

"Then she brought him a drink and a phone number and right after that you guys were gone." Jessica rested a hand on her hip. "What happened?"

She shrugged. "Just time to go."

"Are you leaving?"

Mallory recognized that deep voice laced with lazy amusement and her question was answered. Not only was Caleb Dalton still in the building, he was standing behind Jessica, just a few feet from her desk.

"Hi," she said. "I thought I saw you in the hall a little while ago."

"Yeah. I have errands in town and stopped to see my dad."

"And I just stopped by to let you know I'm going home," Jessica said to her. "If there's nothing else you need."

"Got plans?" Caleb asked.

Jess nodded. "Going to meet friends at the Ace in the Hole."

Mallory wanted to say she hoped her coworker had a better time than she had, but held back. They were in different places in their lives. It occurred to her that Jessica might have chemistry with Caleb. Maybe the receptionist should go with him. Not.

"Have fun," she said instead.

"Thanks. See you around, Caleb."

"Sure thing. Bye, Jess." He touched the brim of his hat.

Then Mallory was alone with him and felt as if she had a lump in her throat the size of a Toyota. But apparently he didn't have any problem talking.

He settled his hip on the only corner of her desk not covered in files and paperwork. "It occurs to me that the Ace in the Hole is a good place for meeting people and having fun but not so much for a first date."

"You would know that better than me." That wasn't being mean or snarky. Just an observation based on what she'd seen and heard.

"I *should* have known," he clarified. "Definitely dropped the ball on that. My dad confirmed just now."

"You talked to your father about it?"

"Yeah. Not that I couldn't figure things out for myself," he added. "Just wanted to make sure he was okay with me asking you for a second date. Since you work for him."

"It wasn't really necessary for you to involve him." This was another first for her—the boss being even peripherally involved in her personal life. "There isn't going to be a second date."

"Can we talk about this? You said we would later," he reminded her.

"That was for Lily's benefit. There's nothing more to say."

"I disagree. Give me one good reason why you won't give me another chance."

She stood up and walked to the far side of the office, where hopefully the spicy, masculine scent of his skin couldn't reach inside and twist her in knots. "I'll give you two."

"Even better. Take your best shot."

"I'm starting the legal process to adopt Lily." She braced for him to turn white, then break a speed record heading for the exit. "Your father is handling it for me."

"Lily's a lucky girl and the two of you couldn't be in better hands. Dad will take good care of you."

"I know."

An unwelcome and irrelevant thought popped into her mind. His father was a good man who had raised him. Would Caleb be like him, take good care of the ones he cared about?

"What's the second thing?" he asked.

"Since Lily came to live with me, my goal has been to make her life as stable as possible. My getting involved with someone could threaten that."

"But I'm her favorite cowboy."

"She's a child. It's not her job to know what's best for her. That's why I'm here."

"And what's best for you?" His blue eyes darkened with intensity. "If you don't make a life for yourself, it will be hard to make one for her. I'm not talking vows or commitments. I just want to take you out for a nice dinner. Not here in Rust Creek Falls. This time we'll go to Kalispell, where no one knows us and we can just focus on getting to know each other."

"That sounds really nice," she said. "But I have to be honest about my concerns. You know I dated someone for several years and it was hard for me when things didn't work out. Then I only had to worry about myself, but what if Lily gets attached to someone and then he's gone? She doesn't need more loss to deal with."

"That's a valid concern," he agreed. "The thing is, though, you still need a life. Lily has to fit into it, and you can't protect her from everything. It's not realistic. She'll grow up without the tools to get herself back up when she's knocked down."

"Kind of like getting back on the horse when you fall off," she mused.

"Exactly."

It made a certain amount of sense. "I never thought about it like that."

"See?" He smiled. "I'm a handy guy to have around."

"Either that or you've been watching too many psychobabble TV reality shows."

"Dang, you got me. I have that portable television in my saddlebags and turn it on every time the cattle let me take a break."

The visual he conjured made her laugh. "Thanks, Caleb. You gave me an interesting perspective."

"And for my reward, will you go out to dinner with me Friday night?"

How could she refuse? And who was she trying to kid? The moment she saw him standing in her doorway, her willpower had disappeared. Her two reasons for refusing to give him another chance were about scaring him away, but he wouldn't let it drop.

Dinner in Kalispell sounded like fun and there had been too little of that for so long now. Besides, neither of them was looking for anything serious. She couldn't really see a downside.

"I'd like that a lot," she said.

"Okay, let's try this again." Caleb opened the door of his truck parked in front of Mallory's house, then handed her inside. "I'm glad you could get Cecelia to watch Lily."

"She said it was no problem."

Mallory remembered what her friend had said after agreeing. There was no man in her life, so at least one of them should have an opportunity for sex. Mallory decided not to pass that on to Caleb. It was her plan to have fun. Not that sex wasn't fun, and if his kisses were any indication, it would be fifteen on a scale of one to ten. But the goal was to keep this simple. Sex would complicate the heck out of it, so that wasn't going to happen.

He slid into the driver's seat beside her and drove away from the house, eventually heading south on highway 424 toward Kalispell as a steady rain began to fall.

He turned on the windshield wipers and gave her an apologetic look. "There are thunderstorms in the area, but I don't want you to worry."

"Why would I?"

"That's right." He nodded as if just remembering something. "You weren't here during the flood last year."

"No, but I've heard stories about people losing everything they had."

"Yeah. It was pretty bad." A flash of lightning revealed his grim expression. "I just meant that the truck has all-wheel drive and we'll be fine if it starts raining harder."

"I appreciate knowing that."

Mallory looked over at his big hands on the steering wheel and the competent and confident way he drove. He was like his father, steady and strong. The kind of man you could trust. Knowing that let her relax, and after a lifetime of independence and only relying on herself, it felt surprisingly good.

Another flash of lightning zigzagged and crackled in the inky sky, and the thread of anxiety always poised inside her threatened to unravel. Then she looked at Caleb, who seemed unconcerned. So she would be, too.

She chatted about weather, work and whatever popped into her head. Even though rain followed them all the way, it felt like no time at all passed before the lights of Kalispell appeared in the distance. Mallory had been here a few times with Lily but didn't know the place well, only that it was quite a bit bigger than Rust Creek Falls.

After exiting the highway and traveling through town, Caleb finally pulled into the parking lot of a place called North Bay Grill. "Here we are."

"It looks nice." The restaurant was on a corner in what looked like a respectable area. The building had wood siding and neatly trimmed flowers and shrubs surrounded it. "Not a neon beer sign in sight."

"If only I could control the weather," he said, watching the hard-driving rain quickly block out visibility when the windshield wipers stopped. "You're going to get wet."

"Not the first time. Probably won't be the last. And—" she smiled at him "—the really important part is that I won't melt."

"Okay, then. Let's make a run for it."

After sliding out of the truck and meeting at the rear end, he grabbed her hand and they ran toward the front door. Without warning he swung her easily into his arms and she let out a surprised, "Oh!"

"Puddle," he explained, splashing through some standing water that was deeper than it appeared.

Her shoes and the hem of her slacks would have been soaked. As she looped her arms around his neck, she said, "My hero."

"Told you I was handy to have around."

Yes, he was, and the reality of it made her want to sigh.

There was an awning over the front door that sheltered them from the rain and he set her on her feet, then grabbed the door's heavy wood handle and pulled it open.

"After you."

"Thanks."

Inside, the lights were dim and strategically placed to illuminate an interior designed to look like a charming New England fishing village. A welcome change from the steak-and-barbecue places she'd encountered since moving back to Montana, Mallory observed happily. Since Caleb had made a reservation, they were immediately shown to a table that just happened to be in front of a fireplace where flames were cheerfully crackling. It felt good on a rainy night but Mallory had a feeling just being near Caleb would keep her warm.

When they were settled with a basket of fresh baked cheddar biscuits, a beer for him, glass of white wine for her and their dinner orders taken, Mallory smiled.

"What?" he asked.

"It's so different from the Ace in the Hole."

"Because no one's looking at us?"

"Or giving you a phone number," she agreed. "Not that the Ace isn't a lovely place."

"Personally I like this small, intimate table with the white tablecloth and candles."

"It is very nice."

"My dad's recommendation." He took a sip of his beer. "He and my mom have been here and like it."

"You're very lucky."

"Because my parents like to try different restaurants?" he teased.

"No. You respect them and value their opinion." She envied him growing up in an environment of support and warmth. "You tease about being forced to have Sunday supper with them, but your mom cares enough to make it a command performance in spite of everyone giving her a hard time."

"I know." Candlelight made his eyes look darker. "I take it your parents aren't that way?"

She shook her head. "It's why my sister left home as soon as possible. And why I have virtually no contact with them even now."

"What do they do for a living?"

"Doctors. My dad is a medical researcher and, oddly enough, my mother is a pediatrician."

"Why odd?"

"Maybe ironic would be more accurate." She met his gaze. "She literally knows kids inside and out. She can diagnose an illness and sees children from birth to teenagers, and establishes a professional relationship with them. But she couldn't relate to her own daughters."

"Obviously you tried."

"Yeah." She twirled her wineglass. "From an early age I realized that going to my parents with a problem was a waste of time and usually an exercise in humiliation. We were expected to handle anything and everything on our own."

"That explains a lot."

"I know, right? Good grades were expected and we didn't let them down. Not then." The really sad part was that the way she'd been raised made it difficult to let anyone in. The lesson she'd learned was that relying on anyone else made her weak and stupid. "My sister left home at eighteen to go to college and I didn't understand why she abandoned me until I was the same age and graduated from high school."

"What happened?"

"The parents who never made time, the same ones not there while we were growing up, were suddenly *there*. Telling me what to do with my life. Where to go to college. They turned their backs on Mona when she refused to follow in their footsteps and go to medical school."

"That's pretty harsh."

"Yeah. Then I got the same treatment. Maybe even a little more pressure because I was their last chance to get it right."

"Since you're not a doctor, I'm guessing you didn't knuckle when they leaned on you."

"No, but of course it was all about me not living up to my potential."

"Not everyone should have children." His mouth pulled tight. "Although in your case I'm glad they did or you wouldn't be here. And I'm very glad you are."

"That's sweet of you to say." She smiled. "But Mona and I talked about that. She desperately wanted children, then adopted Lily and was afraid of screwing her up because of not having a positive role model. Now it's up to me not to screw up."

"Do your parents know about her?"

She nodded and felt the familiar knot of anger tighten. "They didn't exactly welcome her to the family, what with her not being *really* related."

"Their loss." He reached across the intimate width of the table and squeezed her hand. "She's a great kid and you're doing a terrific job with her. Never doubt that. Your parents don't know what they're missing."

"You're absolutely right."

The warmth of his fingers, the supportive touch, were

like life-giving sunshine or a long, cold drink of water when you were thirsty.

He turned his hand so that hers rested in his palm. "Then I'm going out on a limb here and saying that you should trust your gut more."

"Why do you think so?" she asked.

"Because moving to Rust Creek Falls was a good decision. It's not a place where folks let you sink or swim. They pitch in and help out when necessary." He grinned, suddenly and charmingly. "Of course, the flip side of that is everyone knows when you go to the Ace in the Hole and it ends badly."

"Yin and yang. Balance. It's a small price to pay for having people there when you need them." She took a sip of wine. "I feel I should apologize for starting the evening on a down note. That wasn't my intention. And if *this* evening goes badly, I'll take full responsibility."

"Mallory, you don't have to handle anything and everything on your own." He wrapped his fingers around her hand again. "I'm happy to listen and I'm having a great time, by the way."

She smiled. "I'm not sure I believe that, but if it's true, this experience should improve, because I intend to change the subject to something much more cheerful. And it's not about me."

"Oh? What would that be?"

"You." She took a biscuit from the basket and set it on her little plate. "Tell me about growing up in Rust Creek Falls."

He sipped from his beer bottle. "That's not a good idea. It would put you to sleep, which isn't my goal on a do-over date."

"Caleb, I'm serious. I made the decision to pull Lily out of New York, a place that was familiar, and dragged her across the country to what must have felt like the moon to her. It would be reassuring to hear that there's a chance she might not grow up to hate me and end up in therapy because I forced her to move to Montana."

He tried to maintain a properly serious expression but failed when a laugh popped out. "You're very dramatic, aren't you?"

"Is that a problem?"

"Neither confirming nor denying." He nodded approval at her response. "Spoken like the smart, efficient paralegal that you are."

"Being serious isn't the same as dramatic."

"Doesn't make a difference to me." He shrugged. "I think it's pretty cute."

The compliment slid through her and left a trail of warmth in its wake. Not only was he handsome and a cowboy, which was an already devastating combination, but he seemed comfortable with his sensitive side, as well. The total package. In her experience that was rare, but the evening was still young. There was still time for everything to go south and she couldn't decide whether or not she was hoping it would—before she did anything that might complicate her life even more.

"So," she said, "are you going to tell me about your childhood or do I have to get really dramatic?"

"Yes, ma'am. I mean no. But where to start?" He looked thoughtful. "I could be prejudiced, but Rust Creek Falls is the best place in the world for a kid to grow up."

"Why?"

"Prettiest country you'll ever see to run wild in."

"So you were wild?"

"To a point." He grinned. "Remember all those folks who have your back? Well, everyone had my mom's. If I ever got out of line, she heard about it."

"Did you ever get out of line?"

Dumb question. Of course he did. Look at him. Men

wanted to be him and women wanted to be with him. It
had probably been that way since he was a kid. She could
picture him as a mischievous little boy taking every opportunity to push the envelope.

"I plead the Fifth on that. I learned pretty early not to
incriminate myself." He tried to look saintly but only managed to take sexy to a new and complex level.

"I bet your mother had a terrible time with you."

"You'd have to ask her." He toyed with his beer bottle.
"But I wasn't really that bad."

"I just mean that discipline would have been an ordeal.
One minute she probably wanted to wring your neck and
the next you made her laugh."

The corners of his mouth curved up and he looked
pleased. "I think there might have been a compliment buried somewhere in what you just said."

He was right about that. And there was so much more
than his charm that she liked about him. Mallory felt as
if she was caught in an avalanche and tumbling down a
steep mountain slope trying to catch hold of something to
stop herself. It was too fast, too intense.

And it scared her.

As if the angel of romantic complications was watching
over her, the waiter chose that moment to bring their dinner. The interruption took the edge off her serious turn of
thought and for the rest of the meal they talked about nothing important. But even that became significant because he
made her laugh, which took on a great deal of importance.

They finished dinner, shared a piece of chocolate cake
as big as his truck and lingered over coffee. But eventually
there were no excuses to delay leaving and she was sorry
to see the evening end when the server came back with
Caleb's credit card and the receipt to sign. When that was
taken care of, the man started to turn away, then stopped.

"Mr. Dalton, you're from Rust Creek Falls, aren't you?"

"Yes. Why?"

"The thunderstorms are pretty bad, so we've been monitoring the Department of Transportation warnings."

"What's wrong?" Caleb asked, instantly alert.

"There were reports of flash floods, and apparently a section of highway 424 is blocked with debris. It's closed until crews can clear it."

"Any idea how long that will be?"

"Right now they're saying not until morning." The guy looked apologetic.

"Okay." Caleb nodded grimly and stood, sliding his wallet into the back pocket of his khaki slacks. "Thanks for the heads-up."

Mallory slid the strap of her purse over her shoulder. "Now who's getting serious? We'll just take an alternate route home."

"That's the thing." He put his hand to the small of her back, guiding her toward the door. "There's only one route and it's not usable."

"You mean we're stuck here?" How she wished for that charming smile of his that was so comforting.

"Unless we can hire a helicopter, we'll be here at the very least overnight."

"Oh, no—"

Just when Mallory thought things couldn't get worse, the lights went out.

Chapter Eight

Caleb figured it wasn't a good time to point out to Mallory that this was the yang to Rust Creek Falls's yin. It was rural, and a small population made numerous superhighways and roads unnecessary. The flip side of that was when you only had one way out and it was closed, you had to scramble for a plan B. Roads were at the mercy of the weather and their situation was collateral damage.

He'd put Mallory in the truck and turned on the overhead light to minimize the eerie blackness. She looked pale and scared and he could see her starting to shake. The August night was cool because of the rain, but not cold. At least to him. For her reaction was setting in and spending the night in his truck didn't seem like a good idea unless there was no alternative.

"First things first. Let's see if there's cell service. After the flood last year, communications were out, but I don't think this is that bad." He pulled his from his pocket.

Mallory fished in her big purse and came up with her

phone a lot quicker than one would think. She touched a button and the face lit up. "Oh, good."

"Me, too. I need to let Anderson know what's going on, since I'll miss morning chores."

"I hope Cecelia can keep Lily."

"If not, I'll give my folks a call. They'd love to have her."

"I couldn't impose on them."

That stubborn pride of hers and parents who'd made her feel like a failure if she asked for help would make the process of realization take a little longer, but she'd eventually learn to trust. "What part of Rust Creek Falls folks having your back do you not understand?"

There was silence from the passenger side of the truck and when he looked over there was a sheen of moisture in her eyes.

"It's just so hard for me to ask for help, Caleb."

He knew it was dangerous to touch her because he'd want to do more and this wasn't the right time, place or circumstance. But he just couldn't ignore the need to comfort. He couldn't help himself. He reached over and cupped her soft cheek in his palm and brushed a rogue tear away with his thumb.

"That's the thing, Mal. You don't have to ask. Help is just there when needed." He pulled his hand away and curled his fingers into his palm. "And that's how it is growing up in Rust Creek Falls."

"I didn't expect to get such a swift and drastic answer to that question."

Good, he thought. That was more like her. Shock was receding some, letting her natural spunk shine through. "Give Cecelia a call and we'll go from there."

While she called and explained the situation, he talked to his brother. Tomorrow was Saturday and stock needed tending as always but anything more involved waited until the weekend was over if possible. Just like he'd figured, Anderson said they'd manage without him. After promising to keep everyone informed, he hung up. Mallory was still talking to Cecelia.

"You're sure it's not an imposition to stay with Lily? You know day care is closed tomorrow?" She listened and nodded. "Thank you. Really. I owe you. No, I do." Listening and nodding some more, she finally said, "Of course. I'll let you know when we know something about the road opening. I wish Lily wasn't asleep and I could talk to her. Can you have her call me in the morning? Okay. Good. Bye, Cece. And thanks again." She hit the off button on her phone and gave him a remorseful look. "I'm a bad guardian. That's what she's going to think. That I abandoned her."

"I can advise you to stop beating yourself up but before that let me just say—first, you couldn't know this was going to happen. And second, you're allowed to have a life." He held out his hand as if giving her permission. "Although we have better things to do, feel free to commence your guilt trip at any time."

"You're right. And that was a pretty good snap-out-of-it speech. Stuff happens and learning to roll with it is an important lesson for Lily." She sighed. "What better things do we have to do?"

"Find rooms for the night."

"Oh. Right."

Caleb couldn't really blame her for sounding as if she was going in for a root canal.

After several hours and numerous phone calls later, Mallory lost track of how many hotels and motels they'd contacted, driven to and been turned away from. It turned out that in addition to the fact that this was Friday night and people were here for the weekend, the end of summer was fast approaching and last-minute vacationers were in town. On top of that, with the road out, many people were just like them—stuck here and needing a room.

Mallory was tired, frustrated and increasingly glad that Lily was safe, sound and sleeping in her own bed, blissfully unaware of what was going on. If not for Caleb's calm and reassuring presence, she knew she'd be freaking out.

They were now standing at the registration desk of a chain hotel that was pretty much their last hope of finding somewhere to stay for the night. The front-desk clerk, a boyishly good-looking guy in his twenties, was checking the computer for availability. Lights had gone out in the area where they'd eaten dinner, but not all over town. At least not yet. When the guy said "aha", Mallory allowed herself to hope.

"You have two rooms?" That was what Caleb had asked for and she was beginning to give up hope.

"No. Just one." He looked at them. "I'm sorry. It's the only one. Everything else is taken."

Caleb met her gaze. "We can keep looking if you want. There are a few more places we haven't tried." He hesitated for a moment, then continued, "But if they're full, too, and we come back, this room will probably be gone."

Mallory was tired and it was getting late. Storms were still rolling through with rain, wind, lightning and thunder. As awkward as sharing a room would be, it was better than spending the night in his truck. Caleb had his wallet out and was reaching for a credit card. Obviously he was in favor of booking a single room and was just waiting for an okay from her. Given a series of not-great options, this one seemed like the best.

"Let's take it," she said.

He nodded and handled check-in. The clerk gave him two key cards and pointed out the elevator. The good news was they had a room. Bad news was it was on the top floor and the windows faced west, the direction the storms were coming from.

After the ride up, they found the room and Caleb opened the door for her. Just as she walked in there was a bright flash of lightning and seconds later a loud crack of thunder. Mallory flinched, then turned and burrowed against him. Instantly his arms came around her.

"It's bright and loud," he said calmly, rubbing his hand soothingly up and down her back. "But we're inside and safe."

She had a feeling he would be someone you'd want to have around in a crisis. But she was independent and resilient all by her lonesome. Didn't ask for help and didn't need it. The lightning and thunder had just surprised her.

Stepping away from his solid warmth was harder than it should have been given how short a time she'd known him. Still, she had the sensation of wanting to stay close forever. And because she did, it was important to back away.

"Sorry about that," she said.

"I'm not."

The subtext of those two words was that he liked holding her. That was bad because she was counting on him being the neutral one. If his nerve endings were pulsing as hard as hers, she was in trouble. This was going too fast and the intensity of what she was feeling was so much more than she was ready for.

"So, let's see what we've got," she said, flipping the light switch on the wall beside her.

The room was basic: bathroom, desk, small table and king-size bed. She'd been in rooms like this before. With her boyfriend. She and Lily had stopped more than once on the road from New York to Montana. And now she was here with Caleb. He was bigger, broader, more *there* than she'd ever experienced before. It was as if she was in a shoe box with him and there was no place to go where they wouldn't touch.

She looked at the bed again and wondered why it couldn't at least have been a couple of queen-size ones. Her luck wasn't that good. Or maybe that wasn't it at all. If she believed in signs like Winona Cobbs, it would have to be concluded that the universe was pushing her and Caleb together.

"So, I'll take the floor." Mallory saw the look on Caleb's face go from zero to stubborn at her statement. It was sexy for reasons she didn't understand and she wasn't in the mood to explore why that was.

"The hell you will." He settled his hands on lean hips and stared at her. "For the record, I'm perfectly capable of keeping my hands to myself if we shared that bed, but obviously you don't trust me."

She didn't trust herself, but how could she explain something she didn't understand. "It's not that, Caleb, but—"

"It's okay, Mal." He blew out a long breath. "Obviously you're uncomfortable with the situation, and I don't want you to be. It's late. We should get some sleep."

Fat chance of that. But it was a sound strategy and they should at least try.

Mallory took the bathroom first and cleaned up as best she could without her own toiletries. When she came out, Caleb went in. She saw that he'd taken the comforter off the bed and a blanket that had probably been an extra one in the closet and folded them to make the floor a little softer.

Yeah, right. Now she felt worse than awful.

She was standing by the foot of the bed when the bathroom door opened and he came out. "Caleb, we can both sleep in the bed. Put the pillows between us or something."

"I'll be fine. I've spent more than one night on the trail hugging the hard ground. This is an improvement."

"Really?"

"No rocks." He nodded but there was no charming grin. There was tension in his eyes and the hard line of his jaw.

"Oh." She caught the corner of her lip between her teeth. "But you really don't have to—"

"Yeah, I do." There was no easygoing tone in his voice. Just an edge to it, as if he were fighting some internal battle. "Now, go to sleep."

"Okay."

She crawled into the big bed fully clothed and it felt weird. But there was no way she'd take them off. Caleb turned out the light and disappeared below her line of sight. She heard him punch the pillow and thought it was a little harder than necessary. Then everything was quiet.

That didn't last long. There was a bright flash of lightning that showed around the curtain covering the window. Almost instantaneously there was a thunderous boom and she knew a storm cell was practically on top of them. She could picture the forecaster on the news pointing out the orange and yellow on the Doppler radar, colors indicating problem spots that looked so small until you were in the middle of one. That was disconcerting enough and then the electricity went out.

She knew that because the digital clock on the nightstand beside her went dark. There had been a glow coming from buildings around the hotel but it was gone now. Before she could process that, there was another flash and thunder immediately followed. Then it was pitch-black in the room. From sensory overload to nothing was unnerving and she gritted her teeth, trying to hold it together. Even shutting her eyes didn't help because she knew darkness had swallowed her up.

"Caleb," she whispered. "Are you asleep?"

His laugh was ironic. "No."

"The lights are out."

"Yeah, I noticed."

"Okay. I wasn't sure you knew." She'd mostly just wanted to reassure herself that she wasn't alone. It took every ounce of her willpower not to slide out of the bed and curl up beside him on the floor. Just to feel the warmth of his skin and the sound of his breathing.

There was another crack of lightning that was followed by the familiar roar. She pulled the covers over her head and pressed her hands to her ears, trying to block out the sound. A whimper escaped her lips.

"That does it. I'm coming in there with you." Caleb's voice came to her out of the darkness. "I'm not getting fresh. Just so you know."

She lowered the sheet and blanket and heard the sound of him moving toward her. The bed dipped from his weight and relief swept through her.

He'd probably heard the sound she'd made and knew she was afraid. "Thank you."

She didn't care if it made her a hypocrite. She moved close and he pulled her into his arms. With her ear against his chest, she could hear the steady beat of his heart.

"When I was a little girl there was a bad thunderstorm," she began. "It woke me up and I was really scared. I went to my parents' room and tried to crawl into bed with them. Mother told me to stop being a baby and go back to sleep."

His arms tightened around her. "There's a word for women like that, but I won't say it."

His words made her smile. "There's a part of me wanting to make excuses for her, but I can't. If Lily was afraid I'd never send her away."

"Of course not."

"And don't judge. I'm not making excuses for being a wimp now. I just wanted you to know why I react that way to storms."

"It's okay. I'm not judging."

She felt the rumble of his chest. "The thing is, I've gotten pretty good at handling everything that life throws at me by myself. But when disaster strikes, I prefer to have the lights on when I deal with it."

He laughed. "Unfortunately, so often when disaster strikes it usually wipes out all the basics we've grown accustomed to."

"I know." She sighed. "And that's why I'm asking you to stay here. Sleep next to me. Just to keep me from freaking out."

"Okay."

"I could handle it. I've learned how to deal," she assured him.

"No one doubts it."

She wiggled closer to his solid length and rested her arm across his flat belly. "But it's awfully nice to have you here. To not be alone."

"I'm glad. Good night, Mallory." His lips brushed her forehead.

It was like a devil wind driving that single spark into a forest fire. Liquid heat poured through her, along with yearning she'd been trying to ignore since they first met, she realized. She rose up on her elbow and looked down, trying to see, but unable to make out his features in the complete darkness. In spite of that, or maybe because of it, she kissed his cheek. If he didn't want her the way she wanted him, it would just be a friendly, thanks-for-being-patient-with-me kiss. If he did...

Her heart was pounding and she swore there was as much electricity right here in this bed as there was outside. Caleb didn't respond and she was about to pull away—maybe she even moved a fraction—but suddenly he threaded his fingers through her hair, holding her to him.

"Mallory? Do you know what you're asking? If I'm misunderstanding the signal, we can both roll over and go to sleep. I won't leave you." His voice was ragged, showing what it would cost him to let her go. "But if I didn't…"

She settled her hand over his and half turned her head to press a kiss into his palm. "You didn't."

"For the record," he said, "I had every intention of being noble."

"Sometimes nobility is highly overrated."

"Thank God."

The fervent note in his voice thrilled her and washed away any misgivings. This felt so right that she turned off her head and gave her gut instinct free rein. The tension between them intensified in the most exciting possible way as he rolled onto his side and found her mouth with his, as easily as if he had GPS. She kissed him back and melted into him, absorbing the charm, strength and sexiness that was Caleb Dalton.

He kissed her for a long time—her forehead, nose, lips and cheeks. Whispering in her ear, he said, "I've been preoccupied with your neck since the day we met."

"Oh?"

"Yes, ma'am. It's very distracting."

"I'm sorry."

"Don't be." His laugh vibrated against her skin. "It's every bit as soft and sweet as I imagined it would be."

The words were both a dream and a promise—surreal and seductive. "I'm glad I didn't disappoint."

"I don't think that's even possible."

His fingers found the waistband of her slacks and undid the button, then slowly lowered the zipper. She suddenly went hot all over and needed the feel of his hand on her bare skin and helped him along. She wiggled out of her pants, taking her panties, too, then kicked them away before his warm palm rested possessively on her belly.

She held her breath, waiting, wanting, craving. But he didn't go further. Not then, and she moaned in frustration.

"Sweet Mallory. We have all night, you know. We have nowhere to go and no way to get there."

"Thank God," she whispered, echoing his words.

He kissed his way down her throat again and found the ridge of her collarbone, tracing it with his tongue before blowing softly on the lingering moistness. Tingles skittered and danced over her skin and the knot of need tightened a fraction inside her.

Mallory rested her hand on his chest, disappointed that it was still covered by his two layers of shirt, one long-sleeved and the other plain white. She slid her fingers underneath, almost frantic to feel his warm skin. It was covered by a light dusting of hair that felt perfect and, oh, how she would like a visual.

"I wish I could see you."

"I'd give almost anything to see you." He reached under her blouse and gently cupped a breast covered by her bra. "But my hands are drawing pictures for my mind and you are one beautiful lady, Mallory Franklin."

She smiled and kissed his neck so that he could feel the upward curve of her lips and how his words pleased her. "My hands would like to draw pictures, too, but your shirt is in the way."

"Your wish is my command."

The bed moved and cool air crept in when he rolled away. Moments later he was back, reaching for her hand. He placed it on his chest, over his hammering heart. She explored the broad expanse, and the coarse hair tickled her fingers. But oh, what a picture it made in her mind. The contours and muscles. He had an honest-to-goodness six-pack that was nothing like a male model in a magazine. This was real and there was no doubt about Photoshopping, because her hands and fingers didn't lie.

Something else didn't lie. He shifted closer and she

felt his hardness pressing against her thigh, proof that he wanted her as much as she wanted him.

As if he could read her mind, he undid the buttons on her blouse, starting from the bottom and slowly moving up. She held her breath when his efficient fingers brushed by her breasts, lingering for a moment—two—then continuing up to part the sides of her shirt.

He bent and took her breast in his mouth, latching on to her nipple through the silky fabric. So preoccupied with the pleasure pouring through her, she was hardly aware when those clever fingers reached behind her back and easily flicked open her bra.

"I'm doing my damnedest to paint a picture in my head," he said raggedly, "but all this stuff is in my way."

"Can't have that."

Because she desperately wanted the feel of his warm hands on her, she sat up. Eagerly he swept off the rest of her clothes. In seconds she was back in his arms, while his mouth and hands skimmed over her, making magic wherever they went.

And they went *everywhere*.

He snuggled her closer and she could feel the hardness behind the fly of his pants pressed to the most womanly part of her. The picture in her head was erotic and exhilarating, but instinct was saying hurry. Except that would rush things. Like he'd said, they couldn't go anywhere. Wouldn't she be foolish to rush something so wonderful?

"I can hear you thinking," he said.

"And?"

"Stop it."

She laughed and placed a soft kiss on his chest.

"Mallory—"

Her name on his lips was a warm breath against her neck, as if he were branding her, marking her as his. And what had been wonderful just moments ago was moving in the direction of absolutely perfect. He was kissing his way down her shoulder, over her ribs, to her navel.

"Caleb?"

"Hmm?"

He said the single sound against her belly, and the vibration went straight to nerve endings that were swollen and sensitive. Her chest grew tight, so tight she could hardly breathe, hardly talk.

"I really think you should take off your pants now."

His only response was a groan and the mattress moved as he hustled to comply.

"Wait—" She put a hand on his arm, somehow finding it in the darkness.

"What?"

"You do have protection?"

"Yes." Then he went still, as if that sank in. "Not that I planned on this happening. It's just—"

"I understand." She laughed. "There's no way you can be responsible for the road washing out. You're just—responsible."

"Okay, then—" His voice was breathless and sounded almost desperate.

In the dark she heard the scrape of his pants and belt across the sheets. Then there was fumbling, which she was pretty sure meant he was fishing a condom out of his wallet. The tearing of the packet was followed by the sound of his ragged breathing mixing with hers. And then he stretched out beside her and covered her mouth with his.

He continued to touch her everywhere, eagerly exploring the curve of her waist, her breasts and belly, the sweep of her thigh. Part of her wanted him to go on doing that forever. The other part didn't think she could take much more. And he seemed to sense that. His hand settled on her knee and gently nudged it open. As he slid his hand up the inside of her thigh, she rolled her hips, instinctively letting him know what she wanted.

"Oh, Caleb—" Her voice sounded hungry and harsh even to her own ears.

He rolled over her and tucked her beneath him, bracing his forearms on either side of her. She was trapped in the most exciting possible way and couldn't move her arms. So, she lifted her legs and wrapped them around the backs of his thighs.

"Mal—"

He groaned out her name and entered her slowly, letting her get used to the feel of him. She sighed and he went deeper, kept pressing her, filling her. She shifted her hips just a fraction but he knew what she was asking for.

There was no more going slowly. He rocked against her, taking her higher with each thrust, each stroke. Her breath came faster and faster until he reached between where their bodies were joined and caressed the sensitive bundle of nerve endings at the juncture of her thighs.

The touch sent her straight over the edge and she cried out. But he was kissing her and took in the sound of her release, held her until the trembling stopped.

He was still hard, still filling her, and she rocked against him now, urging him on. She went slowly at first, then faster and faster until he groaned out his release and held on to her for dear life.

They stayed that way for a long time and Mallory was reluctant to let go, loving the closeness. The sex was pretty awesome, but this was awesome, too.

She whispered into the darkness something that she probably would never have admitted if the lights were on. "That was simply remarkable."

"Can't argue with that."

Caleb left the bed and went into the bathroom. Moments later he returned and was beside her again, pulling her against him. Taking this intimate step should have scared her but the only scary thing was how safe she felt.

At least she had tonight and the rest could wait until morning.

Chapter Nine

The next morning Mallory woke up in Caleb's arms and memories of the previous night floated through her mind. She was sleepy, satisfied and for several moments felt completely carefree. Sunlight peeked around the curtain covering the hotel-room window. And that was when reality came rushing back. The road was impassable and she was cut off in Kalispell.

"Lily."

An adrenaline rush chased away sleep as efficiently as a caffeine blast. She sat up and the sheet fell to her waist, revealing that she was as naked as after making love with Caleb last night.

This wasn't a great time for an attack of shyness but that didn't stop it. He hadn't technically *seen* everything, since the room had been pitch-black, but he'd sure found his way with his hands. The pleasure of his touch rippled through her even now.

"Mornin'." Caleb had one eye open and his dark hair was tousled from sleep.

He was too cute for words and it was so tempting to slide back under the covers and forget all her responsibilities, just for a little longer. Then guilt zeroed in and she couldn't believe she'd been so selfish. How could she even think that? Lily would be worried and insecure, and here she was just thinking about herself.

"I have to call Lily." With the sheet clutched to her breasts, she looked around. "But first I have to find my cell phone."

Caleb tried the bedside lamp and it went on. "Electricity's back."

He fumbled around and came up with a shirt. "Here."

How sweet was that? He knew she was feeling vulnerable, although the sheet clutched to her chest was probably a clue. She took the garment and slid it on. "Thanks."

"I'm going to find coffee and see if I can get some information on the roads while you talk to Lily."

"That sounds like a good idea."

She slid out of bed, grabbed her slacks, blouse and under things, then went into the bathroom. After washing her face and running her fingers through her hair, she quickly dressed. When she returned, he was fully clothed. He stood there hesitating, as if he was going to kiss her goodbye. As if they'd crossed some sort of invisible line into territory where this—whatever it was—might be more than two people who had turned to each other just because they were marooned together.

In a weird way she was relieved to not be the only one feeling awkward. Especially because Caleb seemed to be the kind of man who didn't feel awkward about anything.

"I'll be back as soon as I can," he said.

"Okay."

When he was gone, Mallory grabbed her phone, found the number in her contacts list and selected it. Cecelia picked up right away.

"Mallory. Are you all right?"

"Yes." Although that depended on your definition of *all right*. "Caleb and I got probably the last room in Kalispell."

"*A* room?" There was a long pause. "You'll have to tell me all about it when I see you."

Mallory decided to let that go for now. "Is Lily all right?"

"Fine. She was kind of quiet when I told her what happened, but I didn't push her. Just let her process the information. We were just about to call you."

"Thank you so much for staying with her."

"Are you kidding? I love spending time with her." There was silence for a moment before she said, "Someone here is anxious to talk to you."

There was a shuffling sound and then, "Aunt Mallory, are you okay?"

"Hi, sweetie." She hadn't missed the anxiety in the little girl's voice and put more enthusiasm than usual into her own. "I'm fine."

"Are you with Caleb?"

Again a particular definition could apply. They were stuck together and had made love, but whether or not she was *with* him was another question. But this child wanted the simple answer. "Yes. The road back to Rust Creek Falls was blocked and right now he's checking to see if it's fixed so we can get back home."

"I know he'll take good care of you." All trace of worry had disappeared from Lily's voice.

"Yes, he will." Still, she should prepare her for all contingencies. "But you might have to stay with Cecelia for a while longer."

"Cool."

"You're okay with that?"

"It's awesome. She said we can go out to breakfast and

get pedicures. Do girl stuff." Lily's anticipation practically vibrated through the phone.

"Okay, sweetie. I wish I could talk longer, but I don't have my phone charger with me and need to save the battery. Tell Cecelia I'll let her know what's going on when I have news."

"Okay. Love you, Auntie Mal."

"Love you, too, sweetheart."

A few minutes after clicking off she heard a sound at the door and opened it. Caleb stood there with a cup of coffee in each hand.

"Room service." He handed one of them to her.

"Smells good." She took a sip. "Heaven."

"So, do you want the bad news first or the good?"

Mallory didn't consider herself a pessimist, but usually wanted unpleasant stuff first, just to make sure she could handle it. "Bad."

He sipped from his cup. "The road isn't open yet."

"Okay. So how is there anything good about that?"

"Crews are working to remove downed trees and debris. It will be passable by early afternoon."

"So, we're still stuck here," she said.

"Yes. But, as I always say, when life gives you lemons, make lemonade."

"I'm not quite sure how to do that."

"I am." He moved close and crooked a finger under her chin, nudging it up until her gaze locked with his. Mischief of the sexy kind sparkled in his eyes. "Checkout isn't until noon."

He took her coffee and set it beside his on the desk. Then he pulled her into his arms and kissed her. Fate was putting her responsibilities on hold. If she was selfish for taking pleasure in that, so be it.

The clothes they'd just put back on came off again and Caleb took her hand, leading her into the bathroom. He turned on the shower, and when the water was warm, he lifted her into the tub and joined her. This time she could see with her eyes and not just her hands. She couldn't touch him enough or look at him enough and he must have felt the same. After putting on protection, he pulled her against him and she wrapped her arms around his neck.

He settled his hands on her bottom and lifted as she wrapped her legs around him. She was slick and ready and he entered her with a single thrust. Both of them were breathless as he drove her higher and higher. Together they stepped over and into release, clinging to each other until the pleasure faded to a warm and lovely glow.

"I had no idea what I was missing," she whispered.

When he set her down, Mallory rested her cheek against his chest. It had been a very long time since she'd been with a man and they said you never forgot. But she couldn't forget what she'd never experienced. And she'd never experienced intimacy as powerful as what she'd just had with Caleb.

Caleb knew that with some women sex was just sex, but Mallory was different. She was a single mom concerned about keeping Lily's life stable. That meant not letting a man in without a reasonable certainty that he would stay. It was a responsibility, one that weighed on him driving back from Kalispell.

It was late in the afternoon now and Caleb stopped by his sister's place. After dropping Mallory off he'd decided to visit his folks before going home and his mom sent him to Paige's with a casserole because she was having a rough day with the new baby, Carter Benjamin. When an infant was fussy, getting a meal on the table could be a challenge, his mom had said. Sutter, her husband, was busy in town, fortunately not in Seattle, where he worked part-time raising horses.

So here he was in Paige's family room, where it looked as if a baby store had exploded. Caleb's new nephew was screaming his head off, and his sister looked close to tears herself.

"I'm so tired," she said, bottom lip quivering. "And he won't stop crying."

What freaked Caleb out was when Carter did a thing where he screamed and shivered and didn't make any noise for a second, then there was a sound that could be heard two counties away.

"I put the casserole mom made in the fridge," he said, putting his words into a pitch she could hear over the baby's cries. "Obviously this isn't a good time, so I'll just—"

"Don't leave me, Caleb." A single teardrop slid down her cheek.

Don't do this to me, he silently begged. He hated to see her upset. There was no question she'd been excited about having a baby, starting a family, and now she was sniffling and about to cry. Men didn't like it when a woman cried and it made no difference that the woman in question was his sister.

"Please. Just hold him for a minute. Maybe five. I need to brush my teeth. And my hair. Sutter will be home soon and he'll think I'm some hideous mythical creature from *Lord of the Rings*."

"He loves you."

That appeared to be the wrong thing to say. Her eyes narrowed. "So, you're saying I do look hideous."

"No." He held out his hands in protest and the next thing he knew, a wiggling, screaming human a little bigger than a football was thrust into his arms. For a tired new mom, she was pretty doggone fast. "Hey!"

"That's what you get for confirming I look like something the cat yakked up." On her way out of the room, she stopped in the doorway. "Speaking of that, Carter just ate and he tends to spit up. It might gross you out but it won't kill you. Don't forget to support his head."

"Wait! I don't know how to do this."

"I didn't, either. Deal with it." And then she was gone.

Oh, boy. The baby's face was bright red and his skinny little legs were kicking like crazy. Caleb tried moving him gently up and down but, if anything, the kid cried harder.

"Guess you don't like that, huh, Carter?" He sat on the couch that faced the stone fireplace with a flat-screen TV above it. There was a baby blanket on the cushion, and logic told him Paige had put the baby there at one point. "How much more ticked off could this make you?"

As it turned out, quite a lot. On his back on the blanket, the pitch of Carter's cries went higher and turned more intense. "Okay, back to the drawing board."

Caleb slid one hand under the baby's head and the other beneath the tiny body. Before liftoff, he made sure the vulnerable body parts were accounted for and supported.

"Look, kid, it would be good if you could cut me some slack," he muttered. "Let's give this a whirl and try not to judge. I'm new at the whole uncle/nephew thing."

He managed to get the baby up to his shoulder, one hand on the head, the other on the butt and back. Carter sucked in a couple of shuddering breaths, then sighed. And was quiet. Caleb held his own breath, waiting for the cease-fire to be over and the wailing to resume. But the kid stayed peaceful and seemed to relax.

Paige immediately appeared in the doorway and walked toward him. "What did you do to my baby?"

"Beats me. I can feel him breathing." He turned his back to her. "Is he asleep?"

"No. His eyes are open." She moved in front of Caleb, an expression in her eyes that was part frustration, part wonder. "How did you do that?"

"Beats the hell out of me. Sorry, Carter. I meant to say *heck*." He looked at his sister. "I guess he just wanted to be upright."

"You don't think I tried that?" She shook her head. "It's like you're a baby whisperer."

"Well, I am pretty good with horses," he said. "Not to brag or anything."

"So not the same thing, Caleb." Her tone brimmed with sarcasm. Then she smiled tenderly at the sight of him holding her son. "You should have one of your own. Maybe more than one."

That would have made him squirm, but he didn't want to rock the boat with Carter. "I don't think that's in the cards for me. It includes marriage."

"So what?"

"That's not for me."

She looked at him as if he had alligators coming out of his ears. "A lot of people we know are happily married. Look at me. I'm happy." Wearily, she plopped on the sofa.

"You don't look happy," he said cautiously.

"You're not catching me on my best day, but trust me. Having a family is all I've ever wanted and better than I thought possible."

He patted Carter's back and paced in front of her. "Yeah, there have been a lot of weddings in Rust Creek Falls recently, but how long will they last?"

"What about Mom and Dad? They've been married a long time and are still like newlyweds. It's embarrassing," she said.

"That was a different time." He'd seen what a bad relationship looked like, too. Take his cousin. "Then there's Jonah. He and Lisette knew each other since they were fifteen and it all fell apart. He hasn't been the same since."

"He's more than our cousin," she said softly. "He was your best friend. The two of you used to be inseparable."

"And I lost him." Caleb would always miss the carefree cousin he'd raised hell with. After his marriage fell apart, Jonah left Rust Creek Falls a sad, bitter and angry man. "More than once he said to me that he grieved the baby his unfaithful wife lost, but the best thing he could say about the divorce was that there were no kids who could be hurt by it."

"Yeah." Paige's gaze settled on her baby. "Still, if you want the brass ring, you might have to go around more than once on the carousel."

If at first you don't succeed, get the stuffing stomped out of your heart again? No thanks, he thought.

The baby was really relaxed and all scrunched up against him. "Is he all right?"

"He's sound asleep." Paige took the baby, who squeaked and squirmed but didn't wake. After settling him on the blanket and snugly wrapping it around him, she said, "Does Mallory Franklin know how you feel about marriage?"

Uh-oh. "Why do you ask?"

"Mom said that you took her to dinner in Kalispell and the two of you were stuck there overnight. And I didn't just hear it from her. Word around town is that the two of you are getting close."

Closer than anyone knew, he thought. He couldn't forget the feel of her naked in his arms or the sight of her in the shower just that morning—slick with water sliding over her breasts and a look of female satisfaction on her face that he was responsible for.

I had no idea what I was missing.

Words like that gave a man responsibility whether he wanted it or not.

"Caleb?"

"I like Mallory," he confirmed. "But we're just friends."

"That's a good place to start."

It was a better place to stay. Caleb refused to believe that his ending up talking to his sister about marriage, family and Mallory was a sign from the universe. He would never in a million years hurt Mallory, or by extension, Lily. He liked being her favorite cowboy. But what had happened with his cousin gave a man pause about taking things to the next level.

So, for everyone concerned, Caleb was convinced that keeping his relationship with Mallory fun and easy was the best way to go.

When Caleb had dropped her off after their adventure in Kalispell, Mallory had the feeling he was distant and distracted. She kept expecting him to cool toward her, so she'd been surprised when he sat beside her in church on Sunday morning. Their thighs brushed and memories of being in his arms swept over her. She was pretty sure God would forgive her for the lapse. Then they'd walked outside together and he'd surprised her again with an invitation for her and Lily to go on a picnic. Since they hadn't yet been to the falls from which the town of Rust Creek Falls took its name, he was going to take them.

From where he parked, Caleb had carried a backpack filled with sandwiches, fruit and bottled water that Mallory put together. They had a blanket spread out on a place in the grass that had a spectacular view of the waterfall and footbridge. After the recent storms, the creek was high, and the sound of the water falling into the pool below was loud.

While she sat on a rock nearby, Caleb was demonstrating to Lily the sideways motion involved in successfully making a stone skip three times over the water's surface. Mallory thought this was about the most perfect day she could imagine. Except, of course, the part where she'd had lusty thoughts about Caleb in church.

"It's all in the wrist," he was telling the little girl.

Lily tried and the smooth rock sank like, well, a stone. "I'll never get it."

"Sure you will." He squeezed her shoulder reassuringly. "Like anything you want badly enough, it takes practice."

The child gave him her most perfect pout. "Why did you want to do it?"

"Because my brothers were good at it." He nudged the brim of his Stetson up slightly and rested his hands on his knees as he bent to meet her gaze. "We spent a lot of time here when we were kids. I'm the youngest boy and I wanted to do everything Travis and Anderson did."

"What about your sisters?" Lily asked. "Did they want to do it because you could?"

"It wasn't important to Lani and Lindsay. I guess it's a guy thing." He gently tapped Lily's nose. "If you don't want to skip rocks, you don't have to."

"Good." The little girl grinned up at him. "But I want to ride horses."

"Then we'll have to do that again soon," he agreed.

"Can we? I'd really like to practice *that*."

"Of course. You just tell me when so I can arrange to be there."

"Cool." Lily was looking at Caleb as if he hung the moon. There was a serious case of hero worship going on, and watching the man so warm and patient with this little girl tugged at Mallory's heart. It occurred to her that a positive male influence in Lily's life could be a good thing. A woman needed a template for the qualities she wanted to look for in the man she'd spend the rest of her life with.

Mallory's own father had been distant, always preoccupied with his work, and she wondered if that had contributed to her disastrous love life with a hospital resident who thought the world revolved around him. It dawned on her that she'd picked a man who was just like her father.

She'd dodged a bullet when he'd dumped her, and maybe she should send him a thank-you note.

Caleb couldn't be more different from that guy. It might explain why her feelings were so different, so intense. She wasn't the type to go to bed with a man she'd known for such a short time, but she had. His captivating qualities had lured her into the shower, too. She didn't spontaneously do things like that. More troubling, she didn't regret it. Being with him made her happy, but…

There always was one.

Caleb was a well-known Rust Creek Falls charmer who didn't concentrate that charm on one woman. He spread it around. Mallory couldn't afford to have illusions because Lily's welfare had to come first. The little girl wasn't subtle about wanting Mallory and Caleb to be a couple and there was no way to keep her from hoping. As the grown-up, it was Mallory's job to make clear that she and Caleb would only ever be just friends.

"Auntie Mal, can I put my feet in the water?"

It was a warm day and she was wearing shorts. Mallory couldn't think of a downside. "Sure. Just don't fall in and get soaked. We don't have a spare set of clothes."

"Cool."

"Don't forget to take off your socks and sneakers. I'll hold on to them for you," she said.

After doing as instructed, Lily waded into the waterfall pool up to her knees. She wandered around, looking for pretty stones and leaving the two adults to watch her.

"She's a great kid." Caleb sat beside her on the rock.

"Yeah." It was far too tempting to lean into him, but that would give just the impression she *didn't* want Lily to see.

"So…" He picked up a blade of grass and rested his elbows on his knees. "Has anyone asked you about our overnight adventure in Kalispell?"

That was one way of putting it. *Wild and sexy night* was more accurate.

"No. But I haven't really seen anyone since we got back yesterday." She thought for a moment. "Except Cecelia. She looked awfully curious but didn't ask."

"Was Lily there?"

"Yes." And the light went on. "She didn't want to bring it up in front of Lily."

"That would be my guess." He glanced at her, then back to the child happily splashing in the water, technically not falling in, but still getting wet. "My mom and sister were asking, and since it's church day and people come together, they're bound to talk. You can bet the story is gaining traction."

"Should I be upset?"

"No. I just thought I should warn you that we're generating rumors around town. Before you can say *Rust Creek Falls,* the word will be that we're serious."

"Oh, my."

"We know that's not true," he assured her.

"Yes, we do."

"It's just a man and woman spending time together and having fun."

"That's right." And she wasn't sure how she felt about the not-serious part being true. Every time they were together, she enjoyed his company more and saw unexpected good qualities emerge. In spite of that, it was probably better for her to be safe than sorry.

He met her gaze. "You've probably been here long enough to know that gossip in a small town is a way of life."

"So far I haven't done anything gossip-worthy. And, as I've never been the subject of talk before, this makes me feel sort of proud."

The comment made him grin. "Folks will shoot the

breeze, so just remember it's no one's business but ours. They want to make something serious out of it when we know we're just having fun."

"Good to know."

"Is Caleb coming over for dinner again tonight?"

Lily came out of the water.

"If he'd like to." Mallory met his gaze.

"I would," he said.

So the subject was changed, but that didn't stop Mallory from mulling it over. What Caleb said completely reinforced exactly what she'd just been thinking about and it was a good thing to know they were on the same page.

Because having sexy thoughts about him in church was just a stone's throw from falling head over heels. Knowing he didn't want that any more than she did and the need to protect her niece from getting hurt should be enough to keep her from making a big mistake.

Should be.

Now all she needed was the effect of Caleb's charisma and charm to begin wearing off. Anytime now would be good.

Chapter Ten

Right after moving to town, Mallory had joined the Rust Creek Falls Newcomers Club in order to meet people. Once a month anyone interested in doing that came to the Community Center to chat and network and, hopefully, bring in more members. So far the group was all women and only the same ones consistently attended meetings. On the upside, she'd made some really good friends. The downside was that tonight those friends were going to interrogate her about Caleb.

There was no doubt in her mind that what he'd told her the other day at the Falls was true. People were talking, and her relationship with the charming cowboy was the number-one town topic. She just wasn't sure what to say when asked.

Definitely it was a bad idea to share the fact that she'd slept with him. It was too personal and there was no way to guarantee the information would stay between friends. Also she would keep to herself that he'd been to her house for dinner a few times. She and Lily enjoyed his company, but that information would fuel unwanted speculation. So she would just go with the truth.

Mallory drove into the Community Center parking lot behind the building on North Main Street. She recognized some of the cars already there and knew the regulars had arrived. After walking inside, she passed the information/check-in desk. The interior consisted of the big, open room used for town meetings and large gatherings. But there were also smaller rooms for more intimate groups, exercise or craft classes, and card games.

There was a room with a window facing the hallway and she could see her friends inside. Two rows of overhead fluorescent lights illuminated the space where six folding chairs were arranged in a circle, and four of them were occupied. Cecelia Clifton, one of the founding members, sat between blonde, blue-eyed Jordyn Leigh Cates and Vanessa Brent. The latter was a gifted artist and looked like a living, breathing beautiful painting with her porcelain skin, wavy brown hair and dark eyes. Beside her was Julie Smith, whose long blond hair was pulled up in a ponytail away from her small face. The style made her big blue eyes look even bigger and highlighted the air of innocence that made everyone in the group want to mother her.

"Hi," Mallory said, raising a hand in greeting as she walked into the room. She sat down and looked at the remaining chair. "Sorry I'm a little late. I had to drop Lily off at her friend's house."

"You could have brought her," Cecelia said.

"She gets bored." Mallory probably should have included her niece. The little girl's presence would have limited the scope of the coming interrogation. "Where's Callie? She's always here before me."

"She called me to cancel because she and Nate have

plans." Cecelia's brown eyes twinkled as if she had a pretty good idea what those plans were.

Jordyn Cates sighed. "So, not only is no one else showing up to join Newcomers—"

"And by that you mean men," Vanessa teased.

"Yes, I do. So not only that, but we're losing a core member to a man. We should change our group name to the Wallflowers Club."

"That's too pathetic." Julie's blue eyes looked a little sad at the idea of that.

"But true," Cecelia agreed. "And the word on the street is that our own Mallory Franklin could be the next one to defect for a man."

"You shouldn't believe everything you hear." Mallory set her purse down beside her on the linoleum floor in an effort to hide her expression, just for a moment.

Julie was to her right. "People are saying that you spent the night with Caleb Dalton in Kalispell."

"Not on purpose." She squirmed as four pairs of eyes focused on her, all of them silently asking for more information. She could do that up to a point. "We went there for dinner. He wanted a place where people wouldn't stare at us and jump to conclusions."

"Funny how the best-laid plans have a way of backfiring," Vanessa commented. "Because people are still gossiping. We're your friends. If you can't tell us the real story, who can you tell?"

"You know there was a storm," she started. "The wind was terrible. Trees and debris were everywhere. The Montana Department of Transportation closed the road until it could be cleared. We couldn't make it back."

"So were did you stay?" Julie looked concerned.

"At a hotel. We got a room—"

"A? As in one room?" Vanessa turned to Cecelia. "You didn't know this? I thought you were taking care of Lily."

"That's true," Cecelia confirmed. "And she was right there when Caleb brought Mallory home. It's not like I could ask for details in front of an eight-year-old."

The four women debated that issue for several minutes and Mallory was glad to have attention diverted from her. But the reprieve didn't last long enough.

"We digress," Jordyn said. She tucked her blond hair behind her ears. "So you spent the night together. And?"

Mallory wanted to tell them she'd prefer not to talk about this. There was nothing to say. Certainly not that there was no such thing as signs from the universe. Or that Caleb had awakened something in her and she wanted to close it back up again. But saying any of that would fan the flames of their curiosity. She really liked and respected each of these women but wasn't accustomed to sharing the burden with them. It was hard to silence her inner child, who was still telling her to handle things alone.

"Mallory?" That was Julie's gentle nudge. "We're happy to listen if you want to talk. Is there anything you want to share with us?"

"Yes." She looked at each of them—all different, all beautiful, all friends. "Something very important happened in Kalispell."

"What?" Julie's eyes widened.

Vanessa's mouth dropped open. "Oh, my."

"Yay, you," Jordyn said.

Cecelia leaned forward expectantly. "I *hope* it's good."

"Very." Mallory tried to look as if she wasn't completely confused about how she felt. "Caleb and I are friends."

Again four pairs of eyes stared at her and it was as if each of them was a balloon in various stages of deflation. They were hoping for more. Mallory understood. She'd want any one of them to fall in love and be happy.

Finally Cecelia said, "Seriously? You spent a whole

night with him. Thunder, lightning, wind. Lives in danger—"

"Dramatic much?" Jordyn grinned at her friend.

"It's a gift." The other woman smiled back. "Now, where was I?"

"Lives in danger," Julie said helpfully.

"Right. Emotions were running high, which is when *things* can happen. When personal safety is at stake it can speed up the natural order of things, if you get my drift."

"I think we all get where you're going with that." Vanessa's voice was wry.

"Am I wrong? Is anyone else surprised that all they are is friends?" Cecelia looked skeptical. "Seems to me that was your status with Caleb when you accepted another date with him."

"Yes. But we're even better friends now." As soon as those words left her mouth, Mallory knew that came out wrong.

Oddly enough, sweet, quiet Julie was the one who ran with it. "Define 'better' friends."

"Oh, you know—" She shrugged. The deafening silence in the room told her that wouldn't fly as an explanation. "Nothing serious. We're just having fun."

"How much fun?" Jordyn wanted to know.

"Look," Mallory said, "you all know that Lily has to be my first priority and I'm trying to give her a stable environment. Caleb isn't a settling-down kind of guy. I know that and he knows that I know. And it's okay because I'm not looking to settle down with anyone. Especially him. He's a good-looking charmer. He's Lily's favorite cowboy, and as long as we keep everything low-key between us, it will stay that way."

"In my opinion," Jordyn said, "it's more about him just being a darn stubborn man."

"Aren't they all?" Cecelia frowned.

"Hmm." Jordyn's eyes narrowed on her friend. "Does that glass-is-half-empty comment have anything to do with Nick Pritchett?"

"What?" Cecelia folded her arms over her chest. "Why would you say that?"

"Oh, I don't know." Vanessa batted her brown eyes. "He's a carpenter. You're a construction assistant. That puts you in the same kind of work. Your paths cross on the job. And possibly other places, too."

"What are you implying?"

"I'm not implying. I'll say it straight out." Vanessa looked around the circle. "I don't think I'm the only one who's noticed that you and Nick have been hanging out a lot lately. And good for you."

"As if," Cecelia said. "If there was anything romantic going on between Nick and me, you all would be first to know. We've been friends for years and that's all there is to it. Not a chance in any universe that it's any more than that."

In Mallory's opinion her friend looked a little wistful about that and she understood the sentiment. She'd only known Caleb for a short time, but couldn't deny the regret trickling through her. All the signs of the universe might be throwing Caleb and her into romantic moments but they'd agreed on the terms of their relationship. And they both had good, sound reasons for the decision.

Anything more than friendship would be trouble on multiple levels.

No one had told Caleb that Mallory and Lily were coming to the Daltons' for Sunday dinner, but he was awfully glad they were there. He'd gone to her house for supper a couple days ago, but hadn't seen or talked to her since. It had been a very long couple of days.

He was just coming in from the backyard after a spurof-the-moment football game with his father and brothers. Suddenly there she was, talking with his mom in the kitchen.

Mallory's shiny dark red hair fell past her shoulders and his hands tingled with the need to hold all that thick silk, drag his fingers through it while kissing her until both of them were hot and bothered. She was wearing white cropped pants and a bright yellow, thin-strapped top that left her arms bare. The memory of how she tasted in that spot where her neck and shoulder met made him shudder with need. The urge to hold her was even more powerful and he realized that one night with her wasn't enough.

His mother's voice dragged him back. "There's Caleb."

Lily ran over and hugged him. "Hi."

"Hey, there, little bit." He hugged her back and saw the soft, tender smile on her aunt's face.

"I came for dinner."

"So I see. And you brought Mallory with you."

"Silly," the girl said. "She brought me."

Lily grabbed his hand and tugged him to where the two women stood by the kitchen island. "Hi," he said to her. "It's nice to see you."

"You, too."

"Let me take your purse, Mallory," his mother said. "While I put it in the living room, would you mind getting these two something to drink, Caleb?"

"Sure. What'll you have?" he asked while she handed off her handbag.

"Iced tea if you have it."

"Coming right up."

"I'd like soda," Lily said.

"A woman who knows her own mind." He winked at her. "I like that."

Mallory laughed. "She has her moments, but you should have seen her picking out her clothes in the morning. It's a very serious decision that includes a lot of mind changing. And, for the record, that's a woman's prerogative."

"Is that attitude, Miss Franklin?"

"Just the truth as I see it." Her eyes sparkled with spirit.

"Yup, definitely attitude," he said.

While he filled their drink orders, Lily asked, "Where are Lani and Lindsay?"

"Shopping, I think."

"Will they be here for dinner?" the little girl wanted to know.

"They will if they know what's good for them." He handed her a glass with the clear soda poured over ice.

"Thank you." She took a sip and grinned. "You're still my favorite cowboy."

Caleb poured iced tea from the pitcher into a glass. "You're only saying that to get on my good side so I'll let you ride my horses."

"No, I'm not." Lily started to shake her head, then stopped and gave him a sly look. "But is it working? Can I? Soon?"

"Sure." He tapped her nose, then handed Mallory her glass. "If it's all right with you."

There was a knock on the door and his mother answered it. He could tell by all the oohing and aahing that carried all the way down the hall who had arrived. The baby. And that meant he and Mallory and whatever was going on between them wouldn't be the focus of everyone's attention.

His brother-in-law walked into the family room carrying a car seat with the sleeping baby inside. Sutter Traub was a couple of inches taller than Caleb's six feet, but muscular. He was a top-notch horse trainer who had loved Paige for a long time. A disagreement with his family had caused a rift and Sutter had left town, stayed gone for five years, leaving his sister confused and heartbroken. But he had come back to help after the flood and the two had reunited and gotten married. They were one of the blissful couples she'd mentioned when he'd brought her the casserole.

Although it didn't make him a believer, the two of them seemed content and happy. Together, they smiled tenderly at their sleeping baby boy. And they weren't the only ones.

Lily set her drink on the kitchen island and beelined for the baby as if he were a magnet. She squatted down to get a better look.

"Careful, Lily," Mallory warned. "He's sleeping. Don't wake him."

"But I want to see his eyes."

"You will soon," Paige promised. "He fell asleep in the car and that won't last. He's due to eat."

"Have you met Paige and her husband?" his mom asked.

Mallory nodded. "At the office. It's nice to see you again. Congratulations on the baby. He's beautiful."

"What does he eat?" Lily gently touched the car seat to rock it.

"Milk. His name is Carter," the proud father answered.

"That's a nice name." Lily couldn't take her eyes off the kid. "He's so small."

"Not as little as when he was born," his mom said.

"He was in your tummy?"

"That's right."

Lily looked up at Paige, then her gaze dropped to his sister's slightly rounded stomach and over to the baby boy. He could almost see the wheels turning. No one would ever accuse him of being intuitive when it came to kids, especially little girls, but even he knew what was coming.

"How did he get in there?" Lily asked with all the innocence and curiosity of an eight-year-old.

Caleb stole a look at Mallory's beet-red face and thought she looked completely adorable. The rest of the adults present stared at her, too, looking amused. All of them were wondering how she would answer that question.

"How about you and I talk that over at home?" she suggested.

"Why can't we do it now? Is this one of those things you hope I'll forget about?"

Wow, she was bright and didn't miss a thing, he realized. Really a challenge, but Mallory seemed up to the task.

Patiently she said, "Sweetie, this really isn't the time or place for that discussion."

"Why not?" The little girl was persistent. "I want to know now."

"Well…okay." She glanced around at the adults and the wheels in her head seemed to be turning, too. She was still blushing like crazy. "Hmm. It's like this, kiddo…" She blew out a breath. "I can truthfully say that of all the things I've anticipated having to deal with since being fortunate enough to have Lily with me, this subject wasn't even on the radar."

"Mind if I try?" Paige asked. "I have teaching cred. I'm a sixth-grade teacher at the school."

"And her kids love her," Sutter added.

"Please," Mallory said. "Simple. Basic—"

"Age-appropriate. Gotcha." Paige crouched down to the child's level. "Okay, Lily. This is how Carter got in my tummy. Sutter and I love each other very much. When a man and woman feel that special feeling, he plants a seed inside her and that grows into a baby."

"We planted seeds at day care," Lily shared. "Carrots came up. Is it like that?"

"Sort of."

Again Caleb could see Lily thinking that over and anticipated the next question. Judging by the fact that all the adults observing were trying to stay serious, they knew it, too.

"How does the seed get into your tummy?"

"It happens when the man and woman are alone," Paige said calmly.

Caleb had heard his father and brothers come in from the backyard and sensed when the three of them joined the group. He glanced at Travis, who stood beside him.

"What happens?" Travis asked, clearly not having a clue what this conversation was about.

"Putting a baby in a lady's tummy," Lily answered. "Aunt Mallory and Caleb were alone when the storm got them stuck in that town." She looked up at both of them. "Are you going to have a baby? I want one."

If he'd been drinking anything, Caleb knew he'd have choked, and the shocked expression on Mallory's face told him she was reacting the same way. Fortunately, she'd set her tea on the island. Now it would be good if someone would say something to cut the awkward silence. So much for not being the center of attention.

"Nah, babies tie you down," Travis said. "Can't get one of those car-seat things on a horse."

"I like babies," Lily argued.

"Really? Why?" His brother clearly wasn't concerned about regaining favorite-cowboy status. "They're time-consuming, noisy and they stink."

"Sort of like cattle." Paige stood and gave her brother a wry stare. "Only smaller and more lovable."

Normally Caleb was the one who made a wisecrack about being tied down. He had once taken pride in being a smart aleck on the subject. But not this time. It was a relief and he wasn't sure why he cared.

Travis looked sheepish. "Hey, I'm not the only one who feels that way. Caleb does, too."

Before he could answer, his sister took a step toward their older brother. "Don't drag Caleb into this."

"Why the heck not?" Apparently Travis didn't know when to cut his losses.

"Because of what he did the other day." There was an expression close to adoration in Paige's eyes.

"What did he do?" Mallory asked curiously.

"He stopped by last week with a casserole mom made and I was having a bad day. Carter wouldn't stop crying and I was at my wits' end. All I wanted to do was brush my teeth, so I handed him the baby."

"And you took him?" There was awe in Travis's voice.

"She didn't leave me any choice."

"That's not the point," Paige continued. "Suddenly it was quiet and I was almost afraid to see what had happened. But Carter was fine. He calmed down and went to sleep while Caleb was holding him."

"By the way, she submitted your name for sainthood," Sutter teased.

"Aw, shucks. It was nothing."

But that was not what he saw when he glanced at Mallory. The look of approval on her face made him feel as if it was really something. He was beginning to realize that only she could bring out this feeling and he was starting not to mind.

Since getting to know Mallory and Lily, the idea of settling down wasn't as ridiculous as it used to be. Normally after taking a woman out a few times and, yes, sleeping with her, he was planning an exit strategy before things turned into a relationship.

But Mallory was different. He knew because of how he'd felt when he saw her here earlier, and *pleased* didn't begin to describe it. All he knew was that he was getting in deeper and he wasn't at all sure how he felt about *that*.

Chapter Eleven

It was Tuesday late in the afternoon. Earlier in the day Mallory had turned down Caleb's invitation to take her and Lily out for dinner. The two of them were now on the way to Kalispell Center Mall. School would be starting in a few weeks and new clothes to wow new classmates were practically a rule, a Franklin family tradition in the making. On top of that, Halloween was just around the corner and the beginning of their first holiday season in Rust Creek Falls. She wanted it to be perfect, the bar by which all holiday seasons would be measured from now on.

She'd told Caleb about the shopping trip and he'd offered to drive them. It was so incredibly tempting to invite him along. Everything was better, brighter, more fun when he was there. But something had made her tell him this was a girls-only trip.

They were nearing the Kalispell city limits when Mallory realized she'd been very preoccupied with thoughts of Caleb, and Lily hadn't said much.

"Isn't it fortunate that Mr. Dalton let me off work a couple of hours early so that we could have a girls' night out?"

"I guess."

Mallory glanced in the rearview mirror at the little girl in the rear passenger seat. "Aren't you excited about getting new school clothes? And shoes? You love shoes. Something that sparkles and lights up when you walk. Boots, too. It will be cold before you know it. But I draw the line at those shoes with the wheels in the heels. The ones that let you roll when you lean back. If you ask me, that's an accident waiting to happen. Call me overprotective, but—"

"Aunt Mallory?"

"Yes?"

"You're really talking a lot."

"Am I?" Of course she was. It was hard to talk about Caleb with her niece and not remember just the night before last when the little girl had said the two of them should have a baby. In front of his family. That tended to get her nerves in a panic.

"Yes, you are. But I think I know why."

"You do?"

"Uh-huh. You wish Caleb was here, too."

Mallory glanced in the mirror again and met that serious, dark-eyed eight-year-old gaze. How could Lily possibly know that?

Best not to admit or acknowledge the subtext of that statement, which was that Lily wished he was with them. It was kind of astonishing how quickly he'd become important, and not just to her niece. The situation worried her.

"Isn't it fun to have a girls' day out?" she asked.

"Yes, but—"

"No buts. We're going to have a wonderful time. Just the two of us." You could never go wrong with a little retail therapy. Right? Right.

Mallory left the highway and drove through town to

Kalispell Center Mall and parked near Herberger's, the biggest anchor store. They exited the car, then went in and followed the signs to the girls department. As she'd hoped, once they started looking at jeans, skirts, tops and accessories, Lily was distracted and her mood lifted.

When she'd collected an armful of clothes, she directed the little girl to a dressing room and went in to supervise the trying on and determination of the correct size.

"You're growing too fast," she said, hanging up a too-small pair of jeans. "I think you have to stop eating so much."

"You're silly, Auntie Mal."

"And you're not supposed to get so big." Which of course was a fib. She wondered if every mother had the same feeling—helping her child to grow at the same time wishing it didn't have to go so fast. She handed over a black three-tiered skirt and studied the length when Lily had it on. "Looks good to me. What do you think?"

"I like it."

"Me, too. But in the winter you'll have to wear tights. We'll get some while we're here. Probably black. And we'll look for shoes." Mallory made notes on the spiral notebook she'd brought. Then she handed over a black-and-gray long-sleeved ruffled top and smiled when it fit perfectly. "Don't you love when an outfit comes together?"

Lily grinned and turned away from the mirror to grab Mallory around the waist. "It's my favorite."

"Good."

"I love you."

"I love you, too—" There was a lump in her throat and Mallory had to stop talking. She squeezed the little girl close for a moment, then swallowed the powerful emotions. "Let's get busy, sweetie. We have a lot more to try on."

Several hours later they put many, many bags in the car,

then headed back into the store unburdened. "Now we'll get something to eat before we tackle shoes."

"Can we go to Dairy Queen?"

"You're reading my mind." Winona Cobbs would be proud. "We'll take a shortcut through Herberger's."

"Okay."

When Lily slipped her hand into Mallory's, she felt that pesky lump in her throat again. Emotion expanded in her chest and squeezed her heart. This little girl meant the world to her and she would do anything in her power to make Lily happy.

Hand in hand they walked through the store, sticking to the main aisle. Almost to the exit leading to the mall, there was a display of girls' dressy dresses. Lily stopped dead in her tracks to look at an off-white, full-skirted, lace-over-satin sleeveless dress.

"I love this," she said.

"It's very beautiful," Mallory agreed. "But you don't have anywhere to wear something like that."

"A flower girl could wear it." Serious dark eyes looked up at her. "For a wedding."

Mallory's heart squeezed again, this time with an emotion more complicated than love. How did you protect the child you cared about so much from something that wasn't within your power to make happen? Even if you wanted it.

It probably wasn't politically correct, maternally speaking, but dodging the subject seemed like a really good idea. "Are you hungry, sweetie? I'm starved."

And now she was sending the subtle message that food could be used as a coping mechanism. That was a hill to die on another day. "Let's go eat."

Fifteen minutes later they had burgers and fries and a booth at the mall's Dairy Queen. With any luck the vanilla milk shake Lilly had requested would distract her from Caleb not being there and flower-girl dresses she would never wear in his wedding to her aunt. There was a subject on her mind that was much more important.

"Lily, there's something I'd like to talk to you about."

"Okay." She took a bite of her burger.

"You know that your parents made me your guardian, right?"

"Yes," she said with her mouth full.

"What you might not know is that I really love taking care of you. And I'm talking to Mr. Dalton about making it permanent."

Lily blinked at her. "How?"

"I want to adopt you. Legally." Mallory dragged a fry through ketchup, over and over. "What would you think about that?"

She grew very still and thoughtful. "Does that mean you'd be my mom?"

"It does. But only if it's okay with you," she quickly added.

The little girl smiled an adorably happy smile, as if the weight of the world lifted from her small shoulders. "It's okay."

The feeling was contagious because a great weight lifted from Mallory, too. "Okay, then."

"Will I be able to call you Mom?"

"I'd like that very much."

"Me, too." She took a sip from her milk shake and looked thoughtful. "I bet Caleb likes ice cream. I wonder if he ever went to Dairy Queen."

"My guess is he has."

"I bet he would like that flower-girl dress on me."

"Lily—" *Welcome to the roller-coaster ride called parenthood,* she thought.

"If you and Caleb got married, I could wear it to the wedding. You're going to be my mom and Caleb could be my dad."

Mallory lost her appetite and put her burger down. "Lily, sweetie, you know that a man and woman need to be in love to have a wedding."

"And a baby. Like Carter. Although a little sister would be nice," the girl said helpfully.

Her face burned at the memory of that conversation in front of Caleb's family. She'd wished the earth would open and swallow her whole. Or maybe a black hole that would let her go back in time and change the conversation.

"Lily, I want to make sure you understand that Caleb and I are just friends."

"Friends can fall in love."

It was possible, unless the friends were Mallory and Caleb. But how did one explain that to an eight-year-old who was hoping for them to be a bride and groom?

"I know you like Caleb, ladybug—"

"Don't you?"

"Yes." Very much. Too much. It would be so much easier if she didn't like him at all. "But we're not the kind of friends who are going to get serious."

"But it could happen."

"No, it can't. Caleb and I talked about it and we're just not going to be a couple." When disillusionment spread over Lily's little face, Mallory wished for another black hole and another change of conversation. But wasn't it better to make her aware of reality than to let her go on wanting something that would never be? "I just don't want you to get your hopes up that we'll have a wedding. You have to stop, sweetie."

Lily studied her for several moments, then nodded, but so much for saving her from disappointment. Mallory felt awful, as if she'd single-handedly crushed this child's hopes and dreams forever.

And this was why she'd told him it was girls only. Some protective instinct had kicked in. Sooner or later he wasn't going to be around, and the adjustment would be easier for both of them if they didn't get used to him being around.

This was Mallory's first time volunteering to get the school ready for opening in September. Mostly parents, but also some who just wanted to help out stopped by to pull books and desks out of storage and make sure everything was ready for classes to begin.

Mallory had dropped Lily off at her friend Amelia's house, where her mother was going to look after the girls. Now Mallory was on her way to the elementary school on South Main Street. She pulled into the lot. Then she made her way to the multipurpose room. At the door was a woman in her mid to late thirties and she recognized Vera Peterson from Crawford's General Store. The woman had a son in Lily's class.

"Hi, Vera."

"Mallory. How are you?"

"Good." She looked around. "This is an impressive turnout."

The pretty blonde smiled. "I forgot. It's your first time at an event like this."

Mallory nodded. "Lily started here in the middle of the school year. I didn't want to move her after all she'd been through, but when Mr. Dalton offered me the paralegal job, there wasn't a choice."

"That little girl has had it rough." There was sympathy in the woman's blue eyes. "How's she doing now?"

"Pretty well." If you didn't count her wanting Mallory and Caleb to have a wedding. "She's made friends and is doing great in school. Adjusting. It was a good decision to bring her here."

"I hear you and Caleb Dalton are going out."

Mallory bit her lip. "In spite of what you might have heard, it's not serious." But still her cheeks were getting hot.

"He's a good guy."

"A very nice man."

Vera laughed. "Okay. You don't want to talk about it. I don't blame you."

"I appreciate that." She looked down at the clipboard on the table. "What's your job?"

"Coordinating. I tell people where to go."

Mallory looked around. "I'm not sure what has to be done or even if I'm needed, but happy to help wherever."

"Amen. Folks here in Rust Creek Falls have strong opinions on things and don't always agree on issues, but when it comes to the kids, everyone is on the same page. They're here to assist the janitor in cleaning up the school, and the teachers are directing decorating their classrooms for the first day."

Mallory hadn't lived in New York all that long, but the place seemed big and busy. There was probably a lot of volunteering, but she hadn't seen it. But then she'd had a lot to deal with helping Lily over the loss of her parents.

"So, tell me where to go."

Vera glanced around the room, assessing the pockets of volunteers with their team leaders. "Looks like Paige Traub could use another set of hands."

"Paige is here?"

"Yes."

"With the baby?"

"Her mom has Carter. Paige is on maternity leave but is supervising her substitute teacher in getting the classroom ready for the first day."

"That's dedication." And the way the woman had been singing her brother's praises as the baby whisperer, Mallory was surprised the new mom hadn't left the infant with his uncle Caleb. "I'll be happy to join her group. Nice to see you, Vera."

"You, too. Don't forget to have fun," the other woman advised, a twinkle in her eyes.

Mallory threaded her way through the crush of volunteers and saw Paige across the room. Moving closer, she could see the sixth-grade teacher with a woman and a man. Then the crowd parted, revealing who that man was.

Caleb.

Her heart skipped two beats, then started racing. It truthfully had never crossed her mind that the carefree bachelor cowboy would be here, although now she vaguely remembered him mentioning the event.

"Hi," she said, joining the group. "Vera Peterson sent me over here."

"It's good to see you, Mallory." Paige gave her brother a funny look. "Let me introduce you. This is Beth Harmon." The other woman was short and had on black square-framed glasses. "And you know Caleb."

If sleeping with him during a thunderstorm qualified, then she knew him pretty well. "Nice to meet you, Beth. I'm Mallory Franklin."

"Okay, let's get to work," Paige said briskly.

She assigned Beth to the bulletin board just outside her classroom door and promised to supervise the message to be displayed. Then she would organize and inventory books and classroom supplies to see what, if anything, needed to be ordered.

Finally she looked at Caleb. "I've saved the best job for you."

"I'm going to hate this, aren't I?" He folded his arms over his chest.

"*Hate* is such a strong word...." She grinned and there was evil around the edges.

"Get out while there's still time," he whispered to Mallory.

"I heard that," his sister said.

Mallory felt it. His breath tickled her ear and sent tingles down her neck.

"You sound just like a sixth-grade teacher," he grumbled.

"I am a sixth-grade teacher. If you were one of my students, you'd spend most of your time in the principal's office."

"Someone has to keep the chairs warm."

"And someone has to wash all the desks," she said.

Mallory leaned closer to him and stated in a loud whisper, "You really should quit while you're ahead, hotshot."

Paige grinned at her. "How much time did you spend in trouble?"

"None." She glanced up at Caleb and thought, *Until now*.

"Okay, then you're partnered with the detention magnet there. Keep him in line." She pointed at her brother, then gave the other mom a grateful look. "Seriously, thank you for your time and effort. In case you didn't get the word, there will be refreshments in the cafeteria."

Caleb put his hand to the small of her back. "Come with me. I know where the buckets and soap are."

"What are you doing here?" she asked as they fell into step and left the big, open room.

"Came to help out."

"But why?"

"My mom made me."

She snapped her fingers. "That's right. I forgot you're afraid of your mom, even though she's the nicest woman in the whole world."

"I'd appreciate it if you would keep that our little secret." He put a finger to his lips in a "shh" gesture that was so darn cute.

The idea of a big man like him being afraid of anything was funny because his strength and confidence made her feel protected. He'd been a rock the night of the thunderstorm.

"Your secret is safe with me." She made the my-lips-are-sealed motion. "But seriously, Caleb, why? You don't have children."

"It's all about community spirit, I guess. Pride in our town and the next generation who will take over and run it. And family." He was quiet for a moment as they passed classrooms where volunteers were mopping floors and putting up bulletin boards. "Anderson and Travis are doing their bit. They're covering for me on the ranch so I can be here and make sure Paige has enough help."

"It's nice of you." She met his gaze. "And don't look now, but it's not a secret that you're a nice guy."

"How do you know?"

"Vera Peterson said so when I walked in today. She sent me over to Paige."

"I see." There was an odd expression on his face.

"Is something wrong?"

"Nothing." He stopped at a door in the back of the building. "We'll find what we need in here."

There was a rolling metal bucket with two compartments and they filled one side with soapy water and one with plain water for rinsing. Caleb found sponges and rags for drying, then they headed back to Paige's classroom.

He pushed the bucket into the room and over to the grouping of four desks by the window. There were messages in pencil. A heart with initials inside—H.R. plus T.D. Smudges. Fingerprints. "I'll wash, you rinse."

"Okay."

They worked in silence for a while but it wasn't the kind of quiet that needed to be filled with words. She just liked being with him, watching the muscles in his arms bunch in the most appealing, masculine way. It made her feel fluttery inside, all gooey and breathless. She'd never experienced this sensation of happiness and contentment at just being with a man.

"So, how was shopping?" he asked.

"Hmm?" The question pulled her right out of that place where everything was fuzzy, gold and shiny.

"You and Lily shopping for school clothes. How did it go?"

Not well, after she made the little girl promise to stop getting her hopes up for a wedding. "We did what we went there to do."

"So it was successful."

"Yes." Sort of.

"Did you miss me?" His sudden charming smile could captivate a room.

Since she was the only other person in it, color her captivated. But no way would she tell him how much both she and Lily had missed him. "It would have been nice to have someone to carry the bags. And there were a *lot* of bags."

"Good." He moved to the second set of desks and started washing dark marks off the surface. "Did you notice the conspiracy today?"

"What?" She was going to get whiplash from subject-change velocity.

"Just now. When we broke down into groups. We were thrown together."

"I was hoping that was my imagination." She'd ignored it, but apparently Lily wasn't the only one pushing for a hookup.

"They can't help themselves, I guess." He looked up from the job. "The flip side of community goodwill is pressure to be a couple."

"Nothing is perfect," she said.

"That's for sure." He met her gaze and the expression in his eyes was impossible to read. "I just didn't want you to feel uncomfortable since we know we're just friends."

That was his way of reminding her they would never be more than that. Sometimes she forgot, but reality always returned.

But, darn it, if the universe would just stop throwing them together, life would be so much easier.

Chapter Twelve

Every Monday Mallory dropped Lily off at Country Kids Day Care on North Pine Street, then went up to Cedar and left on North Broomtail Road, where Daisy's Donuts was located. As much as she liked her boss and her job, it was still *Monday,* the beginning of a long week, so she treated herself to a latte.

She parked and walked inside, deciding that it was almost impossible to be down about anything with the sweet smell of specialty coffee and doughnuts flooding your senses. The little shop had a low counter with a cash register where someone took orders and on either side of it were higher display cases with doughnuts, muffins, coffee cake and scones.

Mallory recognized the two young women behind the counter wearing T-shirts with the Daisy's Donuts logo on the front. Both were college students home for the summer. Carol Tobin, a tall, blue-eyed blonde, was cleaning up and refilling supplies during the morning rush. Kristie Kenmore, a curvy brunette with completely adorable freckles and big turquoise eyes, was working the register.

She smiled. "Hi, Mallory. The usual?"

"Good morning." Her usual was a chocolate mocha, sugar-free, fat-free, no whipped. For some reason, today she was in the mood for everything she didn't usually have. That probably had something to do with Caleb, although she couldn't put her finger on exactly what was bugging her about him. But lately she'd been going with her instincts and decided to do that now. She shook her head. "Sugar, fat and whipped. And a shot of caramel for good measure."

"Wow." Kristie's eyebrows arched questioningly. "Throwing caution to the wind?"

"Yup. Flying by the seat of my pants."

"Large to go?"

As she normally got a middle-of-the-road medium and was breaking all the rules today, she said, "Yes."

"Coming right up." The young woman wrote on the cup and handed it to her coworker, who started making the drink. Then she rang up the sale and Mallory gave her the money. As fate would have it, the correct change.

"Thanks." Kristie smiled. "Good way to start out the week."

"I absolutely agree."

Mallory would take all the good she could get. Since seeing Caleb on Saturday, she'd been out of sorts. Something was off and she was irritated, disturbed.

Caleb hadn't said anything to change the rules. In fact he'd noted the town conspiracy to push them together and wanted to make sure she wasn't uncomfortable with the obvious pressure for them to be a couple. That was possibly the problem; she was conflicted about what she wanted from him. Yet she didn't want to do anything to jeopardize their friendship, for Lily's sake as well as her own.

The other complication was that she worked for his father. She didn't think Ben Dalton would get involved in anything personal between his son and an employee, but why take the chance? Especially when she and Caleb had already hammered out the parameters.

If only she could forget that single night in his arms and stop wishing for just one more.... The feeling of safety, security, of not being alone had been almost as seductive as the man himself. And he was awfully sexy. When she was with him, the sun was brighter, the sky bluer and the thunderstorm had lost its power to panic her. She'd never met a man like Caleb. He was the whole package—handsome, charming, smart, hardworking, loyal, honest.

Also a risk. One she wasn't willing to take.

"Here you go, Mallory." Kristie placed her cardboard coffee cup on the counter, safe in its protective sleeve.

"Hmm?"

"Your order is up."

"Oh. Thanks, Kristie." She smiled and took her latte. "You and Carol must be getting ready to go back to college soon."

"Yeah. One more week and back to the books." Kristie wrinkled her nose, drawing attention to the freckles she despised because they made her look twelve.

Kristie didn't realize that as one got older anything that preserved a youthful look was to be treasured. Mallory felt as if she'd never been young, except when she was with a certain charismatic cowboy.

"Mallory?"

"Hmm?" She met the young woman's gaze. "What?"

"Are you all right?"

"Yes."

Kristie looked doubtful. "It seems like you have something on your mind."

"Always," she said.

"It wouldn't have anything to do with Caleb Dalton, would it?"

"Why do you ask?" As soon as the words were out of her mouth, she knew it was a stupid question.

"The word is all over town." Kristie leaned a hip against the low counter. "That there's going to be a wedding."

Mallory had a bad feeling about this. "And who's getting married?"

"Funny." Kristie's laugh was young and carefree. "You and Caleb, of course."

"Who told you that?"

"People are saying he's really serious about you." The young woman shrugged. "I heard you two are almost inseparable. At church, sitting together at Winona Cobbs's lecture. According to Jessica Evanson, he drops by the law office a lot more than he ever has."

Mallory couldn't deny any of the above, but their relationship wasn't what it looked like.

"So, tell me, how does it feel to snag Rust Creek Falls's most eligible cowboy?"

"I wish I could tell you." She measured her words, choosing them carefully, trying to keep it light. Because, like everything else, her response would be chronicled. "But I haven't snagged anyone."

"You and Caleb *aren't* an item?"

Mallory didn't like that she felt responsible for Kristie's disappointment. People shouldn't have expectations. That realization made her answer very important. Quite possibly she could nip this rumor in the bud, before it circulated through the general population of Rust Creek Falls.

"I'm sorry to disillusion you, but Caleb and I aren't an item. We're friends. I like him a lot, but not in a romantic way." That last part, added for effect, felt so wrong and untrue that she could almost feel her nose growing. But she wouldn't take it back and undo what she was trying to accomplish.

"Too bad." Kristie's mouth turned down in a pretty pout. "You two make a really cute couple."

"That's flattering, but…" She glanced at her watch. "Wow, it's getting late. I have to get to work."

"Have a great day."

"Thanks."

It would be a good day if this gossip about her and Caleb and a wedding stopped right here. He'd made his feelings known and they included being single and unattached. If he heard this, there was no telling what kind of pressure he would feel. Surely no amount of talk could make him care about her the way she would like him to.

And then there was Lily to consider. If she heard this, it would get her hopes up for a wedding that wasn't going to happen. That child didn't need another disappointment in her life. Or another abandonment. If Caleb suddenly disappeared, there could be a serious setback in Lily's emotional recovery from the loss of her parents.

Mallory would do everything in her power to keep that from happening.

Caleb hated mucking out stalls. It was a dirty job but someone had to do it. His brother Anderson felt they shouldn't ask the hired hands to do anything a Dalton wouldn't do, and it was Caleb's turn, so here he was.

The thing about shoveling dirty hay into a wheelbarrow was that it gave you time to think. And right now he was thinking about Mallory. Hell, he thought about her even when he didn't have time to. She continuously distracted him. Her easy smile, pretty auburn hair and lips that tempted a man to kiss her until she melted against him.

It was Thursday and he hadn't seen her since Saturday when they'd volunteered at the school. Today Anderson had gone into town for supplies. If Caleb had been handed the chore, he'd have taken advantage of the opportunity to stop in at his dad's office to say hello to Mallory. Washing desks in his sister's sixth-grade classroom was about as tedious as mucking out stalls, but Mallory had been there with him. Close enough that he could reach out and touch her. That day he wasn't forced to imagine the sweet, floral scent of her skin when he brushed up against her.

Then he'd said something about the conspiracy to throw them together. Pressure to be a couple when the two of them knew they were just friends. After that her brown eyes weren't as bright and her smile wasn't as quick and easy. She'd withdrawn a little. Unlike shoveling the muck out of dirty stalls and laying down fresh hay, women were damned complicated.

Behind him he heard the slow, steady sound of a horse's hooves and looked over his shoulder. Anderson was leading his horse, Cinnamon, into the barn and walked him to the stall Caleb had just cleaned, beside where he was now working.

"Hey," he said. "Done for the day?"

"Yeah. Unless one of those pregnant cows decides to give birth during the night. Or Daisy foals. She's overdue."

Cowboys rode fences twenty-four hours a day to check on the land and animals. He and Anderson had a rotating schedule to share the inconvenience of getting a call in the middle of the night because there was an emergency that required attention.

His brother removed the horse's saddle and draped it over the fence separating the stalls. He unhooked the bridle and slid the bit out of Cinnamon's mouth, then took it to the tack room to hang it up. When they'd first learned to ride a horse, their father had taught them the importance of caring for their animals and equipment. It was something Caleb intended to pass on if he ever had kids, an idea which lately had crossed his mind more seriously than ever before.

Anderson returned with a brush that had coarse bristles and started the process of brushing down his horse.

"Everything go okay today?" Caleb asked him.

"Yup. Can't complain."

"Winter will be here before you know it." Caleb dumped a shovelful of stuff into the wheelbarrow.

"Yeah. We'll be ready."

"Are you going to the church dance tomorrow night?"

Anderson was about an inch taller than Caleb's own six feet and had the Dalton brown hair and blue eyes that could send a clear message when he was annoyed. He stopped the mesmerizing downward motion of the brush and gave Caleb a look that was both annoyed and clearly indicated he would rather poke a sharp stick in his eye.

"No" was all he said.

"Your loss."

"I take it you're going." His brother resumed dragging the brush over the horse's side and back.

"Yup."

"Of course. Don Juan Dalton wouldn't pass up an opportunity to romance the ladies."

His brother never failed to give him a hard time about dating a lot of women. The thing was, playing the field had lost its appeal since he'd met a certain paralegal who worked in his father's office.

"What do you think of Mallory Franklin?"

"Don't know much about her. Do you?" There was a skepticism in his look when Anderson lifted his gaze from what he was doing. And the slight emphasis in the words when he'd voiced the question came across as a warning.

"I know she took in her orphaned niece and is raising her. Doing a darn fine job of it, too. Dad likes her or he wouldn't have invited her to dinner. Twice."

"Looks like you've already made up your mind about her. It doesn't matter what I think."

"No, it doesn't."

Although, next to his father, his brother was the man he trusted most, the man whose opinion mattered a lot. And based on past experience, when Anderson made up his mind about something, nine times out of ten he was right. But Caleb wasn't going to tell him so.

Anderson brushed Cinnamon's flank, then walked around his rump to do the horse's other side, putting his back to Caleb. "Mallory seems to be sticking longer than your usual flavor of the week."

If anyone but Anderson had said that, Caleb might have taken it as criticism, but his brother knew him pretty well. And *flavor of the week* pretty well described his pattern, up until now. But he knew pretty well, too, that Anderson had a more cynical attitude toward the opposite sex. No one in the family knew why he didn't trust women, but his behavior clearly said that was the case.

"I enjoy her company," Caleb finally answered.

"Are you sweet on her?"

"She's different." He shrugged. "I'm not ready to ease on down the road yet."

Anderson turned and met his gaze, a warning expression turning his eyes a darker blue. "Then you should know what I heard in town."

That sounded ominous and grated on his nerves. Caleb stopped shoveling and rested the tip of the tool on the ground. "I know exactly what you heard. The people in this town aren't subtle. And, for the record, I don't need to be warned. Just because you don't trust women, that doesn't mean I shouldn't."

"What makes you think I don't?"

"Hey, this is me. I go out with a lot of different women,

but you hardly go out at all. It's not like you have warts on your nose and a hump on your back."

Anderson glanced over and grinned. "Are you giving me a compliment?"

"No." Caleb leaned the shovel against the fence and grabbed the pitchfork to snatch up clumps of clean hay and spread it over the bare floor. "Just saying that if you showed a little encouragement, there isn't a female in Rust Creek Falls who wouldn't go out with you."

"I don't think Etta Martinson would be so inclined."

"That was a general statement," Caleb clarified. "And Etta is eighty-nine years old. Seriously, Mom and Dad are getting worried about you."

"They worry about all of us."

"That comes with the job description. But they're really concerned about you."

"Why?" he asked sharply.

"Because you're the oldest and getting to the age when people start asking questions."

"Like what?" Anderson's voice had a defensive note in it.

"Like why aren't you married or at least in a long-term relationship."

"It's none of their business." His brother turned and revealed a scowl on his face.

"People, especially here, have a way of deciding what is and isn't their business."

Anderson absently rubbed the horse's back. "You're right about that. And they're pretty interested in what's going on between you and Mallory."

"I know. But out of curiosity, what have you heard?" Caleb looked at his brother.

"When I went in to Crawford's General Store yesterday, Vera Peterson said Mallory had told someone who passed it on to someone else who told her that the two of you are *definitely not* serious."

Emphasis on *definitely not*.

Caleb experienced a quick jab of anger along with something else he'd never felt before. His heart jammed up against his ribs and every beat was painful. A fact he thought best to keep to himself.

"It's nice to know that the Rust Creek Falls grapevine is as efficient as ever."

"Hey, little brother, no need to bite my head off."

So much for hiding his feelings. "That was sarcasm."

"Yeah, and I'm Little Bo Peep. Now, *that's* sarcasm," Anderson said. "Don't kill the messenger. I'm just passing along what I heard. Watching your back as always. And I'm still waiting for you to say that Mallory isn't wrong about the two of you not being serious."

That was because Caleb didn't know what they were. He wanted to lash out at Anderson and say *Don't do me any favors,* but common sense got in the way. That wasn't a bad thing. If the situation was reversed and everyone in town was talking about his brother, Caleb would pass on what he'd heard.

All he could manage now was "I appreciate your concern."

Mostly that was true.

"Anytime, bro." Anderson finished brushing the horse and turned so that they were eye to eye. "I'm throwing a steak on the grill. Want to stay for dinner?"

"No, thanks."

"Got a date?" One of Anderson's eyebrows lifted questioningly.

"No." But he didn't add more.

"Okay." He headed out of the stall. "See you tomorrow."

"Right. 'Night."

Caleb was glad to be alone. His brother knew him too

well and he wasn't sure he could continue to hide the fact that what Mallory said had bothered him. She'd put it out for public consumption that she had no special feelings for him. A good deal of mad was getting up a head of steam inside him, but it was mixed up with something new.

Hurt.

That was bad. For the first time ever, a woman had touched his heart and it confused him. As good a reason as any to explain why he was annoyed that she was repeating to people—who would surely repeat it themselves— what he'd been preaching from day one about not getting serious.

It was time he and Mallory had a talk.

Chapter Thirteen

On Friday night Mallory walked into the Community Center alone. Caleb had called to invite her to the dance but she'd turned him down. It was one of the hardest things she'd ever had to do, but they weren't serious or exclusive and she needed to start behaving that way. He seemed to take it in stride; in fact she'd been a little disappointed that he hadn't tried a little harder to convince her to change her mind. She would have caved, so it was probably for the best that he hadn't.

However, standing in the doorway as she listened to music provided by a Kalispell DJ who'd been hired by the Women's Auxiliary, she fervently wished he was there beside her. The lights were just the right amount of dim and there was a good turnout. It wasn't as if she didn't know anyone. Across the room Jordyn Leigh Cates's blond hair stood out like a beacon and Cecelia Clifton was with her. Probably more of the women from the Newcomers Club were in attendance. Jessica Evanson, the receptionist from work, was there.

Couples were dancing in the center of the room. Ben and Mary Dalton. Collin and Willa Traub were wrapped up in each other. Nate Crawford had his arms around Callie Kennedy and they only had eyes for each other. It made her want to sigh.

Mallory had more friends in this room than she'd ever had in New York, so there was no reason on earth to feel like a stranger who needed a reassuring presence beside her. She simply wanted to be with Caleb, so much that the feeling confirmed her survival instinct in telling him no was right on. She could so easily fall for him even though he'd been completely honest and up-front with her about just wanting to have fun. Her own manicurist had said that he moved from woman to woman, which left out any possibility of commitment, let alone marriage.

She smoothed the front of her black-and-white cotton summer dress and tugged at the hem of the short-sleeved yellow sweater over it. Black sandals with a princess heel completed the outfit she'd obsessed over. It shouldn't be too dressy or too casual. Because even though she'd declined Caleb's invitation, she couldn't help wanting to look her best.

After scanning the room without spotting him, she wasn't sure whether to be disappointed or relieved. But she couldn't stand in the doorway all night and so headed to the folding chairs lining the wall on the other side of the room where she'd seen her friends.

"Hi," she said to Jordyn and Cecelia. "I know I saw the other newcomers."

"They're dancing." Cecelia nodded toward the crowded floor.

Mallory noted that her friend was wearing makeup,

which was an occurrence worth mentioning. "You look beautiful."

"I feel weird." Looking awkward and uncomfortable, Cecelia slid her hands into the pockets of her black slacks. A simple black-and-white print silk shirt was tucked into the waistband, accentuating her trim waist and shapely legs. This was a lot different from her usual uniform of jeans and a T-shirt. "Jordyn did my makeup and made me wear this stuff. And my feet hurt."

"If you didn't want to, then why did you come?" Mallory asked. "Other than to meet *people,* of course."

"I talked her into it." Jordyn looked unapologetic. "But not just so we could huddle together like motherless monkeys if no one asks us to dance. I'm not completely selfish."

"She said I owed her," Cecelia grumbled.

"For what?" Mallory wondered what could possibly coerce her into this transformation.

"Well, there was this blind date I set up for her with one of the guys from the construction crew."

"That doesn't seem like a blackmail-worthy offense," Mallory said.

"Trust me, it was. Disaster," Jordyn said. "Nice-looking guy, but he had the personality of a doorknob."

"Not at work," Cecelia defended. "Just with you."

"So you're saying I bring out the worst in men?" Jordyn's voice was teasing.

"No, I'm saying there was no chemistry." Cecelia shrugged. "But nothing ventured… You have to kiss a lot of frogs before finding your prince."

Mallory's experience with Caleb couldn't have been more different from her friend's. Buckets full of chemistry bubbled over between them from the moment they'd met. And, at least for her, it showed no sign of drying up anytime soon. And kissing? In her estimation, he'd never been a frog. When his lips touched hers, he'd been Prince Charming in a Stetson.

"So, where's Lily tonight?" Cecelia asked.

"She's at a friend's house. Sleepover."

"Speaking of sleepovers," Jordyn said suggestively, "where's Caleb Dalton?"

"I don't know." Mallory wondered when her friend had become a mind reader. "Why?"

"Seriously? You can say that with a straight face?" Jordyn's eyebrows lifted in surprise.

"Of course."

"What's going on?" Cecelia demanded.

"Nothing. That's what I've been trying to tell you. We're just friends."

"You spent the night with him in Kalispell." Cecelia folded her arms over her chest.

"We've already been through this. It wasn't planned," Mallory protested. "And you were with Lily, so you should know better than anyone that we were stuck."

"I'm glad I didn't get stuck with my blind date," Jordyn muttered.

"I heard that." Cecelia grinned. "That's what I get for trying to help."

"And don't think I don't appreciate it. But maybe that's a lesson for all of us that a relationship can't be forced. It has to happen organically."

"I think you're talking about fate." Mallory had had a lot of experience with that lately.

"Don't look now," Cecelia whispered, "but Caleb Dalton just walked in the door and he's headed this way."

Mallory's heart started to dance and her pulse was tapping out the beat. She forced herself to be still and not turn. There was an awful certainty in the pit of her stomach that if she looked at him, everything she was trying so hard not to feel would be there on her face for all the world to see.

Moments later he joined them and stood between Mallory and Jordyn, close enough to feel the heat from his body and smell the spicy scent of his aftershave. "Good evening, ladies."

"How are you, Caleb?" Cecelia smiled.

"Just dandy. You all are looking lovely tonight." He settled his gaze on each of them in turn, letting it linger on Mallory.

Her skin tingled as if it was a caress. And she felt compelled to say something. "Cecelia looks especially pretty, doesn't she?"

"Yes, ma'am." He studied her friend more closely. "What's different—"

"Don't start with me." Cece was used to working with men and had no problem putting one in his place.

"I wouldn't dream of it." He smiled down at Mallory. "Would you like to dance?"

More than he could or *should* know. "Sure."

He touched the brim of his Stetson. "Ladies."

"Don't bring her home too late," Cecelia said, brown eyes twinkling. "Oh, wait, Lily's at a sleepover."

Not helping, Mallory wanted to say, but when he settled his hand at the small of her back to guide her out to the dance floor, the warmth of his touch rendered her utterly speechless.

They found a spot at the edge of the dancers, and when a slow song started, he lifted her hand into his, slid his arm around her, pulling her closer against him. He took charge and there was no question about who was leading, but the truth was crystal clear to her. She would follow him wherever he wanted her to go.

"It feels like I haven't seen you for a long time," he said against her hair.

"Really." Mallory was pretty sure that despite his easygoing appearance, Caleb was uncharacteristically tense about something.

"Yeah. How's Lily?"

"Great. She's at her friend's. Sort of a last hurrah for the summer. But the truth is she can't wait for school to start."

"I remember how that feels."

She laughed. "You make it sound like that was a hundred years ago."

"It feels that way."

There was a serious note in his voice, also unlike him. "Did you like school?"

"I was good at it. But give me a horse and wide-open spaces anytime."

"A wild spirit?" she teased.

"No. Just happier outside in the fresh air." He stopped moving and looked down, something hot and intense in his eyes. "Would you take a walk with me? Outside?"

There was that follow-him-anywhere thing again. It was a bad idea, but she couldn't find the will to say no to him now.

"Okay."

Caleb took her hand and led her out the back door, then around the front of the Community Center. They walked to the sidewalk and started strolling up North Main Street.

"Is there something you wanted to talk to me about?" she asked.

"I guess the whole taking-a-walk-outside thing was a clue." In the glow of a streetlight, his jaw tensed. "Yeah, I do want to talk."

"About what?"

"Just making sure you're all right. I heard that you told someone we're not serious." His tone almost said he wanted her to deny the rumor.

"That's right."

"I see." There was the tension again.

"There was speculation that we'd be married soon. I had to set the record straight," she explained. "I thought it would be a relief to you. Everyone seems determined to make more of this than there is. You and I know we're just having fun hanging out now and then."

"Right."

If she was going to set the record straight, this had to be said, too. "The fact is, Caleb, you're not a marrying kind of guy. People do talk and more than one person has mentioned that you don't have long-term relationships. I'm okay with that. For Lily's sake it's best for me to keep things casual."

"Right. Absolutely." He said the right thing, but let go of her hand. "Good, I'm glad you're not upset about anything."

"We should probably go back inside before people start making something into us taking a walk. Before you know it, the rumor will be that we've eloped."

"Can't have that." The words should have been teasing, but his flat tone sucked out any humor.

Mallory wanted to take back this whole conversation. Rewind this episode and go back to where he'd asked her to go outside. Setting the record straight had changed things between them and not in a good way. He'd said all the right words and that should have been reassuring, but somehow it wasn't at all.

Everything felt awful and wrong.

Twenty-four hours after Mallory reaffirmed their status as friendship only, Caleb sat alone in his house watching some stupid house-flipping show on TV. It was Saturday night, for God's sake. He always raised hell, or at least a little mischief on the weekend. Even a date. But the only woman he wanted to be with was Mallory and she'd put up a no-trespassing sign.

The devil of it was that she'd gotten under his skin and he didn't know how to make it go away.

He got up from the leather sofa in front of the flat-screen TV on the wall in his family room. The house was a typical bachelor's space and decorating wasn't a priority. Mallory hadn't seen it; he always went over to her house. But lately he'd had fleeting thoughts of getting her opinion, asking her to help make this a place she and Lily would like. There was more square footage than hers if…

Last night she'd taken the "if" off the table.

"Damn it." He scowled at the room. "She's never even been here and it reminds me of her."

Because he couldn't get thoughts of her out of his head. He could go to the Ace in the Hole, but the place would be full of rowdy cowboys looking to hook up and women looking to be picked up. That wasn't for him. Not anymore. Besides, it was the scene of his first non-date with Mallory and would be full of memories he was trying to escape.

He walked into the kitchen with its sink full of dirty dishes and the used frying pan on the stove. There was no cute welcome sign over the sink or a framed print that said Count Your Blessings—Recounts Are Okay hanging in the nook by the table. It wasn't warm and cozy like Mallory's house but he had a bad feeling that was more about the company than the furnishings.

Caleb pulled a beer out of the refrigerator and twisted off the cap. On the door was a photo of him and his cousin Jonah. It was held there by a magnet that also happened to be a bottle opener. The two of them were a year apart in age and had been best friends growing up. After Jonah married it was rare for them to hang out, but they'd gone to Kalispell and bought the magnet. They'd joked that it would prevent misplacing the beer opener. But that was before Jonah's life had fallen apart.

That was when Caleb could talk to his cousin about anything and everything. He felt like talking now. It had been too long and was way past time for the two of them to catch up.

Caleb picked up the phone and hit speed dial. "It's Saturday night. He's probably out—"

"Hello?"

"Hi."

"Caleb?"

"Don't you have caller ID?"

"Yeah, but—" there was a pause, as if his cousin was leaning back to relax "—I didn't look. I'm working on some building plans."

Jonah was a very successful architect in Denver. But he was also a single guy, Caleb thought. "It's Saturday night, man. How come you're not out painting the town instead of building it?"

"Oh, you know how it is."

The old Jonah would have given as good as he got and asked why Caleb was cooling his heels at home. But this wasn't the old Jonah. If they'd been in the same room, Caleb knew the other man's hazel eyes would be a little sad, hinting at the heartbreak that had made him turn his back on Rust Creek Falls.

He'd married his high-school sweetheart at eighteen. For a few years all had seemed well and happy, until Jonah found out his wife was having an affair. When Lisette got pregnant, he didn't know if the baby was his, but Jonah was determined to support her through it. And that was what he did, until she lost the baby.

He'd been really torn up about it in spite of the circumstances and afterward all the joy seemed to drain out of him. But six years was a long time. Maybe things had changed and he'd met someone.

If anyone knew how a chance meeting could change your life, it was Caleb. "Yeah, I know how it is. How are you?"

"Doing great."

This man was like a brother and Caleb knew he wasn't great. Life for Jonah was about work and there was no one who made it complicated or special.

"How are Aunt Rita and Uncle Charlie?"

"Fine. Your folks?"

"Good. Happy about their new grandson."

"I heard Paige and Sutter had a baby. Congrats to them."

"Yeah, Mom and Dad are bugging the rest of us to get on with it because they want more grandkids."

"My parents have cut me some slack on that." Jonah laughed, but there was a tinge of bitterness. "So, how is it being an uncle?"

"Pretty cool. I actually held him."

"And you didn't drop the little guy?" A trace of the old humor trickled into his cousin's voice.

"I'm told they bounce, but I don't know that from personal experience. He stopped crying when Paige handed him to me."

"One look at that face of yours probably scared him."

Caleb laughed. This good-natured ribbing was a positive sign. "My sister called me the baby whisperer."

"Don't quit your day job."

"Not a chance." Caleb grew thoughtful at the memory of holding the tiny, helpless human being. "But it does make you think about how having a baby changes everything."

"If you're lucky enough to have a baby."

The sadness was back and humming in Caleb's ear. He kicked himself for bringing up the painful subject and resurrecting unhappy memories. "Look, Jonah, I didn't mean to—"

"It's okay."

Caleb didn't say more. His cousin had left Rust Creek Falls so people wouldn't walk on eggshells around him and he wouldn't have to see the pity in their eyes. He could respect that.

"So," Jonah said, "how's everything with you?"

"Great." There was that word again. Even Caleb heard the forced cheerfulness in his voice.

"Why do I not believe you?" There was a pause before his cousin added, "Let's just cut to the chase. What's her name?"

"What makes you think it's a she?"

"So there is a problem."

Caleb had walked into that with his eyes wide open. But the truth was that he'd picked up the phone in the first place because he needed someone to talk to about this.

"Her name is Mallory Franklin. She's a paralegal in Dad's law office."

"And?"

"She's smart. Beautiful." The word didn't do her justice, he thought. "And a single mom."

"How many kids?"

"One. A girl. Lily." Instantly he had a mental image of the pretty little girl on top of a horse, laughing and happy. The vision tugged at his heart. "Actually, she's Mallory's niece. Her sister and brother-in-law adopted Lily from China. Last year they were killed in a car accident and Mallory took her in. She's making the guardianship legal."

"Hmm." Jonah's tone gave no indication of what he was thinking.

"What?"

"Nothing. Just…that's a lot of responsibility to take on."

Caleb knew he didn't have a reputation for being the

most responsible guy, but when someone needed him, he
didn't let them down. Or break a promise. He liked women
and they liked him. Then he moved on. Except this time
something was messing up the natural order of things.

"Mallory doesn't seem interested in anything serious."

"Did she say that?"

Straight out, he thought. Her words weren't vague and
open to interpretation. "Yes, she said that."

"I'm sorry it didn't work out. If anyone knows how
tough that situation can be, it's me."

"Yeah, I—"

"But there's something you should consider, Caleb."

"Go on."

"When I met Lisette, I was fifteen. But I was convinced
life with her was perfect and would be that way forever. I
was wrong. You should consider yourself lucky that you've
gone all these years without getting serious. Hindsight is
twenty-twenty. You're better off not letting any one woman
get to you. In the long run it saves you a lot of grief."

"I'm all for that, but—"

"A word of advice from the voice of experience. If
there's trouble now, it's not a good idea to ignore the signs.
You can paint over it but that stuff has a way of coming
through to bite you in the ass in the future."

"I hear you."

"Breaking up with her was probably for the best," Jonah
finished.

This was a bad time to realize that Jonah might not have
been the best person to talk this over with. Caleb's mood
was more foul than when he'd picked up the phone. He politely thanked his cousin for listening in spite of the fact
that now he seriously wanted to put his fist through a wall.

Break up? There'd been nothing to break up because
Mallory wouldn't let it go that far. If anything, this talk

with Jonah convinced him that he should walk away and never look back.

After all, looking for the next flavor of the week was what he did best.

Chapter Fourteen

"Is Caleb coming over for dinner?" Lily was setting the table and waited for an answer before proceeding.

"No, sweetie."

"But he likes spaghetti."

Mallory lifted the lid on the big pot. She hoped Lily would believe she was checking to see if the water was boiling yet, but mostly she used it as a distraction to get her emotions under control.

The memory of cooking for him came instantly, vivid and painful. The day they'd gone to the waterfall he'd joined them for dinner. He'd had two helpings of her spaghetti and meatballs, then declared himself too full for even one more bite. But when Lily left the room, Caleb had kissed her until she was breathless. His expression took on a hungry look that had nothing to do with food and everything to do with the fact that he wanted her. She wanted him, too. With a desperation she'd never felt before and had a bad feeling she'd never experience again.

But it was becoming clearer every day she didn't hear from him that their brief, bright flirtation was over. She hadn't had any word from him in a week, and the silence shouted that after their conversation at the dance he'd embraced her message about remaining just friends and moved on.

Mallory walked over to her niece and dropped to one knee, taking the little girl's hands into her own. It was best to be honest because kids knew when you were trying to feed them a line of baloney.

"Sweetie..." She looked into the serious dark eyes staring back at her. It hit her every once in a while how exquisite this child was, the dark almond-shaped eyes, sculpted lips, shiny dark hair. Lily was beautiful inside and out. All Mallory wanted to do was keep her safe and happy. The news she had to deliver wasn't going to do that. "The thing is, I don't think Caleb will be coming over anymore."

"Why not? He likes us."

"I'm sure that's true. But—" How did she put this into words this child would understand? Nobody got dumped, because there were no promises made between her and Caleb, no bad guy to focus hostility on. If he wanted to spend time with other women, feelings shouldn't be hurt, because their agreement was all about no strings attached.

Except Mallory *was* hurting. She missed his charming grin, the teasing sizzles of awareness when he brushed up against her doing dishes after dinner. Watching him interact with Lily melted her heart into a gooey mess. He was so patient, funny, wise.

"But what?" Lily prompted, drawing her back into the moment.

"He doesn't have any obligation to us." That sounded cold, impersonal and wrong because time spent with Caleb was just the opposite.

Lily's dark eyes seemed to grow darker, sadder. "I thought you liked him."

"I do. As a friend." She wanted to add more, but didn't trust her voice not to break. When she could speak, she said, "And maybe in a while he might come over for dinner again. It's just that we can't *expect* that he will."

"Why not?"

Again she knew it was necessary to relate the softest possible version of the truth. "Well, it's just that sometimes relationships don't last."

"But he let me ride the horse and everything," Lily protested. "He *likes* us. I know he does."

"And that hasn't changed. He just can't be here all the time." Mallory was absolutely certain her heart was going to break when a single tear slid down Lily's cheek. She pulled the little girl into her arms. "Oh, sweetheart, please don't cry. We don't need a man around to be happy, do we? We're okay just the two of us, right?"

Small arms went around her neck. "We're fine."

There wasn't a lot of conviction in the words, but Mallory would take what she could get. "I love you, ladybug. More than you can possibly know."

"I love you, too, Auntie Mal."

After one last reassuring squeeze, Mallory pulled back. "There's my girl."

"Am I your girl? For real?"

"Absolutely." She swallowed down the emotion that threatened to choke off her words. "When the adoption is final, it will be legal. But no matter what anyone says, in my heart you are my girl. Forever."

"No matter what?"

"No matter what." For just a moment she cupped the small cheek in her palm. "Okay, then, let's get dinner on the table."

"I'll finish putting the plates and forks out."

"What a big help you are, sweetie."

Had Lily so easily accepted the reality that Caleb would no longer be in their lives? If so, she was dealing with it better than Mallory.

"Do you think Mommy and Daddy are in heaven?"

The question came out of the blue like a sucker punch, sudden, shocking, painful. So much for easy. Lily hadn't accepted his absence and had, in fact, returned to a state of insecurity.

Mallory tried to make her voice calm, matter-of-fact. "I'm sure they are."

"I bet they're watching me right now." Lily folded a paper napkin diagonally, making it a triangle. "Do you believe in angels?"

"I do," she said emphatically. "I have a feeling that your mom and dad are your guardian angels."

"What do guardian angels do?" She started to fold the second napkin.

"They watch over us, even though we can't see them."

"And you're my guardian who watches over me, that I can see."

"Right." *Please*, Mallory prayed, *let that be all she says about this.*

"My daddy used to do that when he took me to the park in New York. He guarded me."

"How?" Mallory couldn't manage more than a whisper.

"He lifted me onto the ladder so I could climb up and then go down the slide." Her little finger carefully pressed the diagonal fold. "When Caleb lifted me onto the horse, it kind of reminded me of Daddy."

Mallory turned away so Lily wouldn't see the tears in her eyes. Her throat hurt from holding back the emotions, and the dam was showing signs of strain. This child who fate had treated in the cruelest possible way had been flourishing in the past few months. Mallory had fretted and agonized about whether or not to leave New York and had finally made the decision based purely on instinct. And it had seemed like the right thing to do. After settling into their new life here in Rust Creek Falls, she'd been adjusting beautifully.

Until now.

This wasn't good. Clearly Lily was regressing. For the past year Mallory had walked a fine line between keeping alive the memory of her parents and not talking about them so much that the child's heart wouldn't heal. Mostly she'd taken her cues from Lily, discussing Mona and Bill when the little girl brought them up. And she hadn't for quite a while.

Questions like these had stopped several months after the move, when she'd started school, became involved in town activities and made friends her own age.

"Auntie Mal?"

"Yes, love?" She blinked hard several times, then turned to look at the child.

There was a sad sort of solemn acceptance on that small, beautiful face. "Do you think Mommy and Daddy would have liked Caleb?"

"Yes, I'm sure they would have." Mallory didn't know how much more of this her heart could take. "Why do you ask?"

"I don't know." Lily shrugged.

Mallory walked from the stove to the kitchen table, pulled out a chair and sat down. She had no idea what to do, no childhood template of how to make an insecure child feel safe. Safety was a state of mind that had eluded her until meeting Caleb. Now she was back where she'd started, over her head in uncertainty and all alone with it. The best she could do was go with her gut, let instinct take over.

She lifted Lily onto her lap and cuddled her close. "I'm so sorry that you're missing Caleb."

"I liked when he came to see us. You did, too. And I think you miss him a lot."

Mallory couldn't deny the truth of that, but she'd been so careful to keep her emotions in check. Be upbeat. She wondered what had given her away. "How did you know?"

"Because when he was here you were happy."

Out of the mouths of babes…

This was exactly what she'd feared would happen if she let a man into her life. Mallory was a big girl and it was an acceptable risk. But Lily was a child who'd too recently lost the two most important people in her world, both at the same time.

Mallory hated being responsible for yet another loss, and if she could do things over, she'd never get involved with Caleb Dalton. Because the problem was that she wasn't the only one who had fallen in love—and lost him.

Caleb walked into Crawford's General Store late in the afternoon, but it was early for him to be off work. Anderson was sick of his foul mood and had told him to go and not come back until he could stop biting everyone's head off just for saying hello. The way he was feeling, that attitude change wasn't looking hopeful anytime soon.

It had been over a week since he'd seen Mallory, and every time he thought about her pushing him away, he wanted to rip someone's head off. And he thought about it a lot. Still, he'd have to find a way to put it out of his mind because there was a lot to do on the ranch and it wasn't fair or right to leave his brother a man short.

But right at this particular moment he had time on his hands and decided to come into town and pick up a few necessities. Crawford's had everything from hardware to underwear and lots of stuff in between. This was as good a time as any to browse and work off a little steam. His sisters would call it retail therapy, so he needed for them not to find out.

He walked up and down the aisles, breathing in the smell of leather that filled the place. This was as good a way as any to try to erase memories of Mallory from his mind.

But it didn't look as if his strategy was working.

Everything he saw reminded him of her. Wooden spoons that made him recall watching her stir something on the stove and how sexy she'd looked doing it. Pink boots made him think of Lily and how cute they'd look on her the next time he took her riding. Except there probably wouldn't be a next time. Everywhere he looked he saw Mallory and realized he couldn't escape her because she was somehow a part of him. The problem was there was her and him but no them and she refused to try.

"Caleb?"

He turned away from the display of saddles and bridles at the sound of the little girl's voice behind him. "Lily?"

There she was in her pink shorts, yellow-and-pink T-shirt and pink sneakers with heels that lit up when she walked. Marched was more like it, he thought, as she moved with determination up the aisle toward him.

"What are you doing here, honey?"

"I saw your truck." She stopped in front of him and looked up.

"From where? Aren't you supposed to be in day care?"

"Yes. Aunt Mallory picks me up at five."

That was about a half hour from now. "How did you get here?"

She gave him a "duh" look. "Country Kids Day Care is diagonally across the street. We were outside playing and I saw you. I walked."

"They let you?" Someone at that place was going to get an earful about lax supervision.

"I didn't tell anyone."

"You just left?"

"Uh-huh." She nodded and her shiny black hair swung forward.

"You didn't say anything to anyone?"

"I told my friend Amelia."

"I meant someone in charge," he clarified.

"No. They wouldn't have let me come."

So she'd slipped away unnoticed. The facility should know about this and keep a better watch over the kids in their charge. However, this kid had pretty awesome covert skills and might be CIA material when she grew up.

"So you made a clean getaway."

"I don't know what that means, but—"

"It means we have to get you back before someone has a heart attack when they can't find you." He held out his hand. "I'll walk you over."

"No." Lily backed up a step and put both her hands behind her. "I have to talk to you."

"Okay." He squatted down to her level and looked into those serious, sad dark eyes. "What's wrong?"

"It's about Aunt Mallory—"

For a split second fear shot through him that something bad had happened to her, then rational thought returned. If Lily was at day care, all was normal except that she'd gone AWOL to talk to him. Whatever it was must be pretty important. Important enough to break rules.

"What about Mallory?" he asked.

"You don't come over to see us anymore and she misses you."

"Lily—" Caleb blew out a long breath. "The thing is, stuff doesn't always work out the way we want."

"That's what she said. But don't you like us?"

That beautiful little mouth started to tremble and he prayed she wouldn't cry. Anything but that. Did he *like* them? *Like* wasn't a big enough word to describe his feelings but it seemed pointless to find one that did.

"It's not that simple, honey."

"It is, too." Anger and defiance stiffened her little body. "Auntie Mal laughs when you're around. And you do, too. She likes you. I just know."

She had a funny way of showing it, he thought. "Look, Lily, this is a grown-up problem. It's hard for you to understand." He lifted his Stetson, then resettled it. "Heck, I don't really understand it myself."

The little girl took a step forward and glared at him. "I'm not a dumb little kid, Caleb."

"Whoa, I never said you were."

"You didn't have to. That's how you're treating me. But I know stuff."

"Of course you do. But so do I." He rested a forearm on his knee and studied her.

From the moment he'd met Mallory and Lily at his dad's law office, the little girl had not been subtle in her efforts to push the two of them together. She was really fired up about this now and he didn't know what to say to calm her down. It wasn't just lip service that he didn't understand. Mallory liked him, and he liked her. It should be simple, but it was complicated. To say that would have been talking down to her.

"Look, Lily, I know you wanted your aunt and me to be together, but we don't always get what we want."

"You already said that but you don't know anything," she cried in frustration. "Things change. Good things don't last forever and ever. If you like someone and they like you back, you shouldn't waste it. That's just stupid."

Caleb wished he could take away every awful thing that had happened in Lily's short life. This kid really tugged at him. What she'd been through had made her grow up too fast and she sounded too mature for her tender eight years. Most of all he wanted to assure her it would all be okay, but leading her on would postpone the inevitable and hurt her twice as much in the long run.

The "aha" light came on and he understood why Mallory had been reluctant to start a relationship. The words hadn't really gotten through but he could see the tragedy on Lily's little face. She was still fragile from loss, and without a guarantee of long-term success, there was too much potential for more heartbreak. Mallory was trying to protect this child, and everything in him wanted to do the same.

"Lily, I'd like to make this better, I really would, but I don't think there's anything I can do."

"You're wrong. You broke Aunt Mallory's heart and you have to fix it so she stops crying every night."

"She's crying?"

Lily nodded solemnly. "She doesn't think I can hear her, but I do."

Caleb rubbed a hand over his neck, hating that anything made Mallory cry. He wanted to protect her, too. If someone else had hurt her, he would step in and stop it, but this wasn't like that. It was going from bad to worse and his hands clenched at the thought of Mallory being unhappy. Lily was making this his fault when her aunt had been the one to push him away.

"Honey, I don't want you to be upset, but I'm just not sure I can do anything to help."

"You can, but you just won't." She shook her head and all that straight dark hair swung around her face. "I don't like you, Caleb. You're not my favorite cowboy anymore."

Before he could stop her, she turned and marched back down the aisle, pink sneakers flashing like bursts of anger.

He jumped up to go after her. Somehow he was going to fix this but first he had to stop her and get her to listen.

She stomped right past Vera Peterson and he wondered how much of the conversation the store clerk had heard. But he didn't care enough to stop and ask. He had to get to Lily.

But Vera put a hand on his arm when he would have rushed past her. "Let her go, Caleb."

"No. I have to make her understand."

"Let her cool off first," Vera said kindly.

"If I could just—"

"So, the rumors about you and Mallory are true."

He looked at her and knew he wasn't getting out of here anytime soon. It was beginning to look as if retail therapy was a really bad idea.

Chapter Fifteen

Caleb looked out Crawford General Store's big picture window and didn't see Lily. Was she that fast? The day care was just across the street and she should have been visible crossing Cedar to get back to North Pine Street, where Country Kids was located. He had to get to her.

"Earth to Caleb," Vera said.

"What?" The little girl's anger and hurt were still bouncing around in his head.

He looked at his friend, but right now her blue eyes weren't as friendly as usual. They were standing at the front of the store beside racks of Western shirts, jeans and cowboy hats. This conversation was the last thing he wanted to do. With a sudden move to the side, he tried to move past her, but she was even quicker and stepped in front of him.

"Not so fast, buster."

"Get out of my way."

"In a minute. We have to talk first."

He'd have to be an idiot not to know what this was about. "How much of that conversation did you hear?"

"Pretty much all of it." Vera didn't look the least bit ashamed of having eavesdropped.

"Then you know there's nothing to talk about."

"Oh, please, Caleb. One of the things I always liked about you was that you're smart."

"You mean it wasn't my ruggedly handsome good looks that attracted you?" He didn't feel the least bit funny but cracking a joke, cranking up the charm, was the fastest way to get out of here and find Lily.

"Don't try to distract me." Vera crossed her arms over her chest. "The Caleb Dalton charisma wore off for me a long time ago."

"Okay, then. We have nothing to say, but I have to make sure Lily's all right."

"Not yet. You'll just tell her all that crap about everything's complicated and she's just a kid who doesn't understand. Patronizing. Yada yada."

"I didn't—"

"Yeah, Caleb, you did."

"Then let me just spell it out. I don't want to talk to you about this."

"I can accept that." Vera nodded. "So go to your dad. Oh, wait, he's Mallory's boss. Anderson? Oops, no, he doesn't trust women, so there goes objective input. Maybe your brother Travis—" She stopped and shook her head. "No, not Travis. He's as clueless as you are. I guess you're stuck with me."

"Look, V, Lily is out there on the street. I have to make sure she's okay."

"You love that little girl." Blue eyes widened in surprise.

"I care a lot about her." That was easier than saying the *L* word.

"I can see that. And I'll make this quick," Vera said.

"You need to listen to someone and apparently the universe picked me to get through to you. I accept the challenge."

Caleb settled his hands on his hips. It was a defensive stance, but felt appropriate under the circumstances. "Okay, get it over with."

"Good to know you have an open mind. It has to be said that you are one stubborn son of a gun." She blew out a breath. "So, I say again, the rumors about you and Mallory are true."

"I don't know what you've heard," he answered, proving her point about his stubbornness.

"That you've been spending a lot of time together."

"Yeah, it's true."

"You were stranded in Kalispell and spent the night in the same hotel room."

"Also true." But what happened in that room was too intimate and special to talk about with anyone but Mallory. Vera wasn't getting that out of him.

Fortunately she didn't go there. "You look at her differently than you've ever looked at any woman before."

"I don't know how I look at women." But he knew how he felt. And the way he felt about Mallory wasn't like anything he'd ever experienced before. It was intense and powerful, wonderful and consuming.

Instead of trying to find a way to let her down easily to get himself out, he was trying to find reasons to be with her all the time. Until she'd wanted to cool it. In all fairness, though, he'd mentioned friendship-only first.

"Caleb, you need to face up to the fact that you're in love with her."

"Not me." He backed away. "That's never happening."

"Is this because of Jonah?"

He shouldn't be surprised that everyone knew, but somehow he always was. It wasn't like people hadn't noticed when his cousin left town and didn't come back. Because it was too painful to live with reminders.

"There was never a doubt in Jonah's mind that Lisette was the one, and their marriage still failed in an ugly and public way. He was crushed by what she did to him."

"Different people, different outcomes." She shrugged. "I knew my husband a few weeks and knew he was the guy for me. That was ten years and two kids ago. I fall more in love with him every day. Do we have our ups and downs? Of course. You name a couple and I'll tell you the speed bumps in the relationship. The ones who want to work it out do. If you don't—" She shook her head.

"What's your point?"

Vera stabbed her finger into the air. "You refuse to try at all."

"No, Mallory is the one refusing," he shot back.

"And you're relieved about that because it lets you off the hook." She was relentless. "What happened to Jonah is your excuse not to take a chance."

"Even if I was willing, there's no reason." Frustration knotted in his belly. "She shut me down. Said I'm not marriage material."

"Oh, Caleb…" Vera's voice softened. "She didn't mean that. She knows you're a good man or you'd never have gotten within spitting distance of her little girl. What she said was just a way to protect herself."

"How do you know?"

"Pushing you away puts her in control of the pain. By expecting the worst, and even creating it, she gets to be in charge of when the bad stuff happens. She thinks it will hurt less that way, but from what Lily said, it's not working out as expected."

"When did you become a psychologist?" he asked.

"When I said 'I do.' It's what happens when you're a wife and mother. Comes with the territory." She smiled.

"Mallory loves you. Everyone in town can see it. But you haven't been looking. I heard what Lily said about her aunt missing you. Only a woman in love behaves that way. You're lucky to have found her after all this time."

Jonah had told him he was lucky to have made it all these years without getting serious about a woman. It had saved him a mother lode of pain and humiliation. But the truth was it had nothing to do with luck or signs. He'd just never met the right woman. In that moment it was as clear and bright as a cloudless Montana sky. He had met the one.

Mallory.

Now that he had, he wasn't going to let her get away.

"I'm lucky in a lot of ways. Including that you're my friend." He grinned and gave Vera a big kiss on the cheek. "I'm going to find Lily now and make sure she's okay. Don't try to stop me."

"Would I do that?" Her blue eyes twinkled.

"In a heartbeat. And I'm grateful. Thanks, V."

"Anytime," she said and stepped out of his way. "I'll keep my fingers crossed."

Caleb ran out of the store and to his truck in the parking lot. He came to a dead stop when he spotted the little girl beside it wearing a whole lot of pink and yellow. Definitely not the outfit to wear if you were trying to be inconspicuous.

"Lily, what are you doing here?" He went down on one knee beside her. "I thought you went back to day care."

She shook her head. "I didn't want to get yelled at for running away."

"The way I see it," he said seriously, "you didn't run away—you ran to something. And you're right."

"I am?" Her eyes widened. "What about?"

"I'm the one who made your aunt cry, and that makes me the guy who can fix it."

"What are you going to do?" she asked, a hint of shock and awe in her voice.

"I thought a talk with your aunt Mallory would be in order."

"Right now?" She looked shocked. "But she's at work."

"Good, she's not far away."

Lily threw her arms around his neck. "Oh, Caleb, thank you."

He hugged her back. "Don't thank me yet. I have to get her to listen to me."

"She will." Lily smiled and the hero worship was back in her eyes. "I know it."

"From your mouth to God's ear."

"Okay, I'll go back to day care."

"Not yet. You're coming with me to the law office."

"But I'm already in trouble," she protested.

"Probably. But I'm going to call them on my cell phone right now and let them know you're okay. We'll stop there and explain what happened." He opened the truck's rear door and lifted her inside. "After that, I'm gonna need all the help I can get convincing your aunt to give me another chance."

"Okay." She sat on the seat and buckled herself in. "She listens to me. Can I go with you?"

"We're going to make that happen, kid." He shut the door. "And I hope what you say is true."

Mallory was sitting at her desk staring at her computer screen when Ben Dalton walked into her office.

"Do you have the trust paperwork for the Bartells?"

Her boss leaned a broad shoulder against the door frame. Somewhere in his fifties, he was still trim and handsome. Caleb looked a lot like his dad and would be just like him, one of those men who got better with age.

Would he grow old alone or find someone to share his life with? Someone who wasn't her.

"Mallory?"

"Hmm?" She blinked, then gave herself a mental shake. "Oh. Sorry, I zoned out for a second." The file he wanted. "I didn't put that on your desk?" She could have sworn it was there, but her boss wouldn't be here now if that was the case.

He confirmed with a simple "No."

"I know it's all ready to go." She skimmed through her own upright file holder and found the one he wanted. Barely holding in a groan at her negligence, she said, "Here it is."

Ben walked over and took it from her. "Thanks."

"I'm so sorry about that." *Sorry* was never a word you wanted to say at work and she'd said it twice in the past two minutes. Not good at all.

"No big deal. They're not coming in for a final review until tomorrow. But you know me." He grinned. "Everything needs to be ready for the next day."

She did know him and liked to think they worked well together because she was the same way. Plan ahead so there were no surprises. One of the last things she did every day was go through the upcoming schedule to make sure her boss had what he needed. She remembered doing the next-day-review part, but somewhere between that and the follow-through she'd been distracted.

Probably by thoughts of Caleb. All her planning ahead hadn't prepared her for the surprise of missing him so much she ached from it.

"I'm really sorry, Ben." Apology number three. "It won't happen again. Truly. I—"

"Whoa," he said. "It's not a big deal."

"It is to me. Efficiency is my middle name."

"I couldn't agree more. Your work is exemplary." He

rested the edge of the file on the corner of her desk. "Is everything all right with you? And Lily?"

Other than dealing with the fact that Caleb didn't want to see them, but that was not anything she planned to discuss with his father. Personal life should stay outside the office, especially when your personal problem was with the boss's son.

"All is well," she said.

"Nothing on your mind?" he persisted.

"No more than usual." That was the first time she'd ever lied to her boss and she felt slimy and awful about it. Still, she had to believe it was the wrong thing, right reason. "Why do you ask?"

"Probably just my imagination, but for the last week or so you've seemed a little distracted. Sad."

He was very perceptive. Not easily fooled. She hated that what had happened with Caleb was affecting her work performance. So far she hadn't messed up anything important and she planned to keep it that way. Starting now she was going to get her act together—with as much of the truth as she could give him.

"I've been a little tired." That was true. It was hard to sleep with her heart such a mess. "And I worry if Lily is adjusting all right, dealing with losing both of her parents at the same time. She's just a kid. As we get older there's a better understanding of the fact that losing a parent is inevitable, but we don't expect both of them to go at the same time. So that's always on my mind." She gave him a confident smile. "But don't worry. I'm on it."

"Mallory, I'm not upset with you. On the contrary, you're the best paralegal I've ever worked with." He frowned. "But I also consider you a friend and that's the only reason I asked. Just so we're clear, if I ever have a problem with your work, there won't be any question about it. You'll know."

"Okay. Thanks, Ben." She felt marginally better, but resolved to make sure he didn't ever know it if she was in personal-crisis land.

"Okay, then. If you need to talk, my door is always open...."

The ring of Mallory's cell phone interrupted and she looked at the caller ID. "It's the day-care center."

With a nod of his head Ben indicated she should answer and after picking it up from the desk, she hit the talk button. Before she could say hello, someone started speaking. The words chilled her. "She did what?"

Her heart was hammering as Lily's teacher told her about Lily leaving day care without permission. But Caleb had brought her back and the little girl was safe. Finally there was a request for her permission. "Of course he can bring her here to the office."

She said goodbye and disconnected, then explained to Ben what happened when Lily saw Caleb's truck at Crawford's.

"He's bringing her here," she explained to her boss. "Why would he want to do that?"

"I have my suspicions." Ben's eyes twinkled. "But you'll just have to wait to find out."

The suspense would probably have killed her, so it was a good thing she didn't have to wait very long.

A few minutes after the phone call, Lily marched into her office. "Hi, Auntie Mal."

Mallory went to her and bent to hug her. "What were you thinking running away?"

"I wanted to see Caleb."

Mallory saw him standing in the hall and felt a rush of emotions. Joy at the sight of him. Confusion. Relief that Lily had been safe with him. More confusion about *why* they were together.

"What's going on?" She directed the question to the little girl.

"I was playing outside and saw Caleb go into Crawford's. I just had to talk to him."

Mallory had a pretty good idea what was on Lily's mind. "So, you left without saying anything to anyone?"

"Caleb said the same thing."

"And what did you answer?" she asked, looking up at him.

"They wouldn't have let me go." There was a whole lot of stubborn determination in Lily's voice.

"Of course they wouldn't let you leave. It's their job to keep you safe. Although someone took their eyes off you." She glanced up at Caleb again, torn between fear about what could have happened and a spurt of happiness because she hadn't seen him in what felt like forever. "It wasn't necessary for you to bring her here. I was getting ready to pick her up after work."

"I wanted to. Because what I have to say couldn't wait."

Mallory felt as if her heart stopped for the second time in two minutes. It was impossible to tell what the intensity on his face meant, but she had a pretty good idea that it was personal. The funny thing about hope was that it could be cruel if things didn't work out the way you wanted. She just wished this conversation could happen somewhere other than his father's office.

"Why don't we talk when I get off—"

Ben cleared his throat. "Lily, how about you come with me to my office. There are some games on my computer I think you'd like."

"But, Mr. Dalton, I have to help Caleb talk to Aunt Mallory."

"Well, sweetie, I think he needs to take it from here. We should give them a little privacy." Ben winked at the little girl.

After a moment, Lily smiled and winked back. "Okay. Do you have that game with the animals?"

"If I don't, I'm sure we can find it. She'll be fine with me," he said, looking at Mallory.

"Thanks," she answered gratefully.

Her boss held out his hand to the little girl and she put hers in his big palm and they walked out, leaving her alone with Caleb.

After several moments, she looked at him and demanded, "This is where I work. Why here?"

"Because it's where I first met you and Lily. We've come full circle. Seemed like the right place for the conversation I want to have with you."

"We said everything the night of the church dance." And she hadn't seen him since. "Your disappearance made it pretty clear how you felt."

A muscle jerked in his jaw for a moment. "You wanted me to challenge the fact that you were insisting on nothing more than friendship."

"I suppose so." She knew so. And even if she hadn't just promised herself that there would be no more lies, she saw no point in denying the truth. "Obviously you were completely fine about leaving everything the way it was. The silence on your end spoke volumes."

"I can see where you'd jump to that conclusion, but let me tell you what was really going on."

"Please." She prepared herself for the charm defense. A man didn't stay friends with all his exes without applying it liberally.

"I backed off because I've never felt about a woman the way I feel about you." He took off his Stetson and dragged his fingers through his dark hair. "It's not easy for a man like me to say this, but I was confused."

That admission was a little bit stunning. Caleb had a cocky, confident streak that could be annoying and attractive in equal parts. So confessing that he was confused about anything, especially feelings, sort of disarmed her.

The anger and hurt drained out of her and she asked softly, "Are you still confused?"

"No."

"Why?"

"Because when an eight-year-old goes over the day-care wall to call you on your crap, it puts everything in perspective." He twirled his hat between his hands. "That and the fact that I miss you like crazy. I can't think of anything but you. Anderson gave me the afternoon off and said not to come back until I can quit being so bad-tempered."

"Why were you crabby?"

"Because of you." He threw his hat on her desk. "I've never been more clear about anything in my life than how I feel about you, Mal."

"Oh?" She held her breath as hope expanded inside her. Happy endings always started with hope, she realized.

He nodded and intensity blazed in his eyes. "I want us to be more than friends. I want to be serious and complicated and everything else that comes with it when a man commits everything to a woman."

"Really?" That was all she could say. He was on a roll and she wasn't going to get in his way.

"Yes, ma'am. At Crawford's Lily reminded me that life is short and it's just foolish to waste time. No one knows that better than her." He took a deep breath. "I love her, Mal. I want to be a father to her if you'll let me. It might be wrong to say, but more important is that I love *you*. I want to make a life with you because you are my life—"

Mallory couldn't stand it anymore. If she didn't touch him, she was going to explode. She launched herself into his arms and he caught her. She took that as a sign that he would always be there for her, always catch her.

"I love you, too," she whispered against his neck.

"Do you think Lily would be okay with it if I propose to you?" His breath stirred her hair.

"Why don't you ask her?" Mallory pointed to the doorway, where the little girl was standing, a broad smile on her face.

She ran over and looked up. "I knew you guys really liked each other."

Caleb went down on one knee and took her little hand. "So you're okay with it if I ask your aunt to marry me?"

"I already picked out my flower-girl dress," she said.

"There's one yes vote." He slipped Mallory's hand into his other palm and met her gaze. "Mallory Franklin, will you marry me?"

She worked with words every day. The law was filled with an abundance of language to make a situation unambiguous. Right here, right now, where she worked, there was only one simple word for this all-important question.

"Yes."

Epilogue

Mallory looked at the ring on her left finger, a platinum band with inset diamonds that told the world she was Mrs. Caleb Dalton. It told her, too, because sometimes she had to pinch herself to make sure this was real. Word around town had been wrong, and their wedding didn't happen quite as soon as everyone had speculated. They'd waited until after the holidays. And characteristic of her relationship with Caleb, their wedding plans had changed when a January blizzard pared the ceremony down to a few hardy friends and family. When the weather cooperated, they had a big reception in the town hall.

Caleb had moved into her house in town because it was closer to work and school for her and Lily. His house was rented out to Cooper Manning. The man was somewhere in his thirties and handsome enough to make the heart of any woman not already in love beat faster. The single members of the Newcomers Club were excited. At first. But the guy kept to himself and no one knew how he made a living. In fact, the only reliable information was that he wasn't a fugitive from the law and paid his rent on time.

So, Mallory was in love with and married to the man of her dreams. There was a wedding photo of her, Caleb and Lily on Ben Dalton's desk. Now the three of them were in his office for the final paperwork on the adoption. Caleb had picked Lily up from school and they were waiting for his dad to return from the town hall. The little girl was sitting on his knee.

She turned the wedding picture toward her and studied it. "Mommy?"

Mallory loved being called that and wondered if it would ever get old. "Yes, love?"

"Do you think I'll ever be able to wear my flower-girl dress again?"

Caleb grinned. "Seems like there's a wedding in this town every other week, so I'd say you have a better than even chance. Until it doesn't fit. The way you're growing, young lady, that could be next week. In fact, I've been meaning to have a talk with you about staying my little girl just a bit longer."

Ignoring the last part, Lily said, "When I get married—"

Caleb gently touched a finger to the little girl's mouth, shutting off the rest of the statement. "That's not going to happen until you're at least thirty-five. Because you have to date first and—"

"We didn't," Mallory pointed out. "Not in the beginning."

"That's different."

"How? We kept running into each other," she reminded him. "And when the universe gives you a sign, it's not wise to ignore it."

"The universe better mind its own business. Lily is off-limits. No boys," he said protectively.

"Ew. I don't like boys." Lily made a face, then smiled up at him. "Except you."

"And that's just the way I want to keep it."

Lily rested her head against his shoulder and Mallory's heart melted yet again. It always did at the sight of the big man, so gentle and loving with the little girl who'd stolen both of their hearts. Their daughter finally had a positive male influence, a man with all the wonderful qualities she would one day look for in a husband.

"Sorry I'm late." Ben Dalton hurried into the room and sat in the big chair on the other side of the desk. "Got hung up on a property-line dispute."

"Everything okay, Dad?"

"Fine. Just took longer than I expected." He opened the adoption file on his desk. He looked at his son. "So your name was added to the adoption petition."

Mallory hadn't thought she could love Caleb more but when he'd said he wanted to adopt Lily, her heart had filled to overflowing. She couldn't believe how happy that had made her. Sometimes she questioned it and Caleb kept her grounded in the moment. He reminded her to enjoy the good in each day and not borrow trouble.

"So, we just have to sign?" Mallory asked. "Shouldn't there be a parade down Main Street and fireworks? This is big!"

"That's all you have to do." Ben grinned. "Then the papers get filed and it's official."

Mallory was first and wrote her name on the line indicated. Then Caleb set Lily down and did the same. The little girl looked over the paper, turned to them and grinned.

"Mommy, we both got to change our name to Dalton."

"That's right. We're a family." Mallory liked the sound of that.

"You do realize that anyone named Dalton has to show up for dinner on Sunday." Ben's eyes twinkled.

"That's a real hardship," she teased back.

"Give it time," Caleb chimed in. "It'll get old."

"Not for me. I've always wanted a close family."

"Me, too," Lily added. "Does this mean that Lani and Lindsay are my aunts?"

"It does. Anderson and Travis are your uncles, with all the responsibilities and obligations that come along with the title. And you have grandparents." Caleb was looking at his father, who smiled proudly.

Shyly, Lily looked at Ben. "What should I call you?"

He smiled down at her. "Grandpa has a nice ring to it."

"And Mrs. Dalton is Grandma?"

"She'll love that, Lily." His voice was exceedingly gentle and filled with emotion.

"I'd like that, too." Lily's expression turned serious as she turned to Caleb. "Now that it's legal, I can call you Daddy?"

Caleb didn't speak right away, but there was a suspicious brightness in his eyes as he swallowed once, then again. When he answered, his voice was thick with emotion. "Daddy is my favorite name."

"You know," the little girl said thoughtfully, "I think you're not my favorite cowboy anymore."

"Lily?" Mallory wondered what was going on in that fertile mind of her daughter's.

"Now you're my favorite Daddy."

Tears trickled down Mallory's cheeks but she knew that was just happiness overflowing again. It was practically a daily occurrence since her charming cowboy had gone from maverick to daddy.

* * * * *

*Don't miss the next installment of the new
Special Edition continuity*

**MONTANA MAVERICKS:
20 YEARS IN THE SADDLE!**

*Cecelia Clifton came to Rust Creek Falls hoping to find
true love. Then she fell for Nick Pritchett, the
Thunder Canyon carpenter she's known all her life—
and the man who has vowed never to marry!*

Don't miss

MAVERICK FOR HIRE

by USA TODAY *bestselling author Leanne Banks.
On sale September 2014,
wherever Harlequin books are sold.*

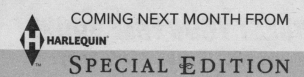
Available August 19, 2014

#2353 MAVERICK FOR HIRE
Montana Mavericks: 20 Years in the Saddle! • by Leanne Banks

Nick Pritchett has a love 'em and leave 'em attitude...except when it comes to his best friend, Cecelia Clifton. When the pretty brunette insists on finding a beau, the hunky carpenter realizes that he can't lose Cecelia to another man. Nick may be Mr. Fix-It in Rust Creek Falls, but his BFF has done a number on his heart!

#2354 WEARING THE RANCHER'S RING
Men of the West • by Stella Bagwell

Cowboy Clancy Calhoun always had room for only one woman in his heart—his ex-fiancée, Olivia Parsons, who left him years ago. So when Olivia returns home to Nevada for work, Clancy is blown away. But can the handsome rancher simultaneously heal his wounded heart *and* convince Olivia to start a life together at long last?

#2355 A MATCH MADE BY BABY
The Mommy Club • by Karen Rose Smith

Adam Preston never worried about babies...that is, until he had his sister's infant to care for! Bewildered at his new responsibilities, Adam asks pediatrician Kaitlyn Foster for help. The good doctor is reluctant to give her assistance, but once she does, she just can't resist the bachelor and his adorable niece.

#2356 NOT JUST A COWBOY
Texas Rescue • by Caro Carson

Texan oil heiress Patricia Cargill is particular when it comes to her men, but there's just something about Luke Waterson she can't resist. Maybe it's that he's a drop-dead gorgeous rescue fireman and ranch hand! Luke, who lights long-dormant fires in Patricia, has also got his fair share of secrets. Can the cowboy charm the socialite into a happily ever-after?

#2357 ONCE UPON A BRIDE
by Helen Lacey

Although she owns a bridal shop, Lauren Jakowski can't imagine herself taking the trip down the aisle anytime soon. In fact, she's sworn off men for the foreseeable future! But Cupid intervenes in the form of her new next-door neighbor, Gabe Vitali. Despite his tragic past, the cancer survivor might just be the key to Lauren's future.

#2358 HIS TEXAS FOREVER FAMILY
by Amy Woods

After a difficult divorce, art teacher Liam Campbell wants nothing more than to start anew in Peach Leaf, Texas. He's instantly captivated by his new boss, Paige Graham, but the lovely widow has placed romance on the back burner to care for her emotionally wounded young son and focus on her career. Still, as Liam bonds with the boy and his mother, a new family begins to blossom.

YOU CAN FIND MORE INFORMATION ON UPCOMING HARLEQUIN® TITLES, FREE EXCERPTS AND MORE AT WWW.HARLEQUIN.COM.

HSECNM0814

REQUEST YOUR FREE BOOKS!

2 FREE NOVELS PLUS 2 FREE GIFTS!

✦ HARLEQUIN®

SPECIAL EDITION

Life, Love & Family

Cecelia Clifton came to Rust Creek Falls hoping to find true love. Then she fell for Nick Pritchett, the commitment-phobic Thunder Canyon carpenter she's known all her life. But when Nick agrees to give his best friend boyfriend-catching lessons, he discovers that there's more to Cecelia than meets the eye—and that he wants her all for himself!

***

"I know these are for the charity auction, but if I give you twenty-five bucks, will you give me a bite of something?"

He must be desperate, Cecelia thought. Plus there was also the fact that she knew that Nick did a lot of charity work. He was always helping out people who couldn't pay him. Her heart softened a teensy bit. "Okay. Two apple muffins for twenty-five bucks. Frosting or not?"

"I'll take one naked," he said and shot her a naughty look. "The other frosted."

His sexy expression got under her skin, but she told herself to ignore it. She handed him a hot cupcake. "It's hot," she warned, but he'd already stuffed it into his mouth.

He opened his mouth and took short breaths.

She shook her head. "When will you learn? When?" she asked and frosted a cupcake, then set it in front of him. "Now that you've singed your taste buds," she said.

He walked to the fridge and grabbed a beer then gulped it down. "Now for the second," he said.

"Where's my twenty-five bucks?" she asked.

"You know I'm good for it," he said and pulled out his wallet. He extracted the cash and gave it to her. "There."

"Thank you very much," she said and put the cash in her pocket.

Within two moments, he'd scarfed down the second cupcake, then pulled a sad expression. "Are you sure you can't give me one more?"

"I'm sure," she said.

He sighed. "Hard woman," he said, shaking his head. "Hard, hard woman."

"One of my many charms," she said and smiled. "You always eat the baked goods I give you in two bites. Don't you know how to savor anything?"

He met her gaze for a long moment. His eyes became hooded and he gave her a smile that branded her from her head to her toes. "There's only one way for you to find out."

***

Enjoy this sneak peek from
MAVERICK FOR HIRE
by New York Times *bestselling author Leanne Banks,*
the newest installment in the brand-new six-book continuity
MONTANA MAVERICKS:
20 YEARS IN THE SADDLE!,
coming in September 2014!

H HARLEQUIN®

SPECIAL EDITION

Life, Love and Family

NOT JUST A COWBOY

Don't miss the first story in the
***TEXAS RESCUE* miniseries**
by Caro Carson

Texan oil heiress Patricia Cargill is particular when
it comes to her men, but there's just something
about Luke Waterson she can't resist. Maybe it's
that he's a drop-dead gorgeous rescue fireman
and ranch hand! Luke, who lights long-dormant
fires in Patricia, has also got his fair share of secrets.
Can the cowboy charm the socialite into a
happily-ever-after?

Available September 2014
wherever books and ebooks are sold.

HSE65838